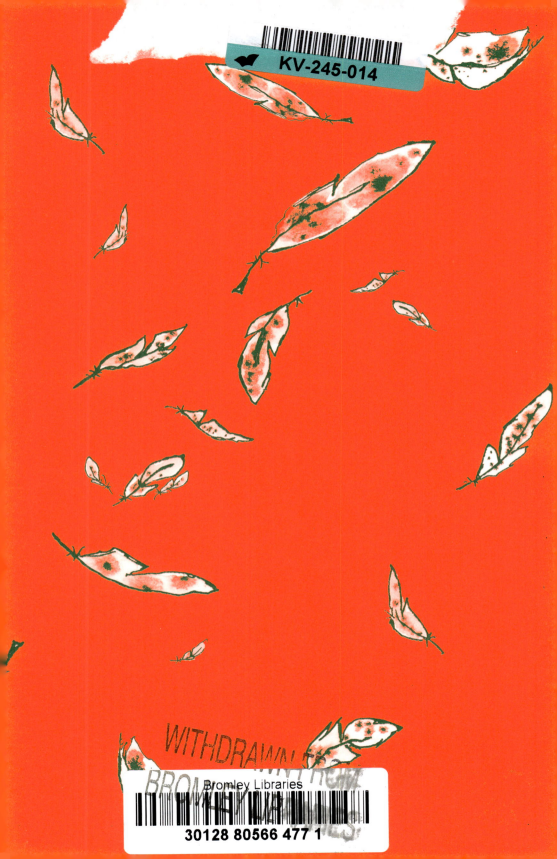

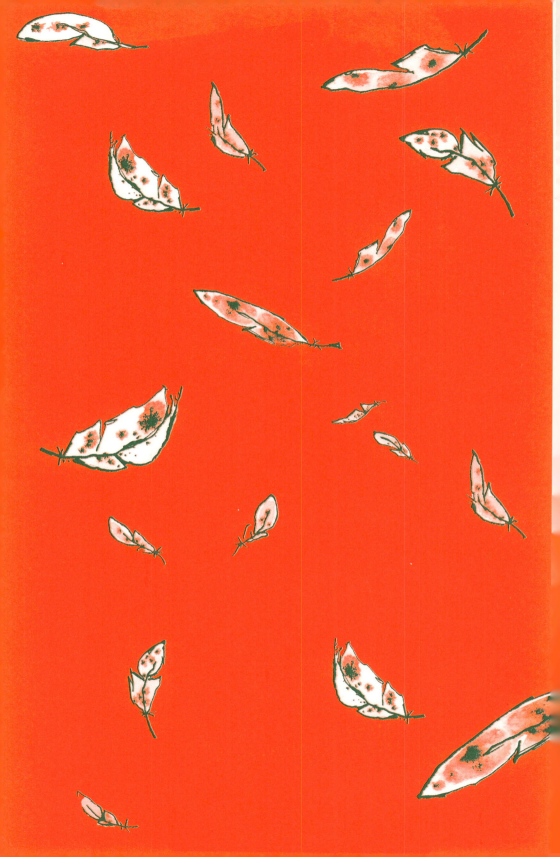

SPY FOX

AND **AGENT FEATHERS**

BY DERMOT O'LEARY

TOTO THE NINJA CAT
AND THE GREAT SNAKE ESCAPE

TOTO THE NINJA CAT
AND THE INCREDIBLE CHEESE HEIST

TOTO THE NINJA CAT
AND THE SUPERSTAR CATASTROPHE

TOTO THE NINJA CAT
AND THE MYSTERY JEWEL THIEF

TOTO THE NINJA CAT
AND THE LEGEND OF THE WILDCAT

WINGS OF GLORY

DERMOT O'LEARY

SPY FOX

AND AGENT FEATHERS

ILLUSTRATED BY CLAIRE POWELL

HODDER CHILDREN'S BOOKS

First published in Great Britain in 2024 by Hodder & Stoughton

1 3 5 7 9 10 8 6 4 2

A CIP catalogue record for this book
is available from the British Library.

ISBN 978 1 444 97646 5

Printed and bound in Great Britain by Clays Ltd, Elcograf S.p.A.

The paper and board used in this book
are made from wood from responsible sources

Hodder Children's Books
An imprint of
Hachette Children's Group
Part of Hodder & Stoughton Limited
Carmelite House
50 Victoria Embankment
London EC4Y 0DZ

An Hachette UK Company
www.hachette.co.uk

www.hachettechildrens.co.uk

To all those who fought

for the liberation of Europe

3 June 1940

Two miles inland from Dunkirk, France

The zip of the bullet passing just overhead was the first sign that things might not be going well for foxes Charles Redfearn and his French cousin Emmanuel.

'*Mon Dieu!* That was close!' Emmanuel laughed, despite the danger. 'Quickly, make for the hedgerow. Do you have any idea why they are shooting at us?'

'Well, I'm glad you're finding it funny!' Charles replied as the pair sped across the fields and another bullet cracked through the air above them. 'I can't even tell who's shooting, let alone why.'

'*Mon cousin*, we are foxes . . . It could be anyone.'

This was true; foxes weren't top of many humans' Christmas card list. But these weren't regular foxes. Emmanuel was one of the top young fighters in the French Animal Army, famed already for his bravery, speed of thought and lightning pace. He was the youngest commando in his unit, an expert saboteur . . . *and* he cooked a mean omelette. His best friend and cousin Charles was just as qualified. Charles was a dashing special agent for the British Special Animal Executive (or SAE), an elite organisation made up of the cream of the animal kingdom. He was an expert in explosives and paw-to-paw combat, had been part of the gold-winning 5000-metre digging team at the 1936 Berlin Olympics . . . *and* he could make a cracking chicken and leek pie.

As soon as war was declared Emmanuel, and most of the animals in his village, signed up to the French Animal Army. They were working day and night to help the humans try and defend their country against their invaders: the German army. Not that the humans had any idea, of

course! Charles had been tasked by his bosses in London to assist his cousin 'in any way possible' and keep tabs on enemy movements. What quickly became clear, however, was that the German army was a fierce enemy. Their tactics had taken everyone by surprise and now British and French soldiers – both human and animal – were retreating to the French port of Dunkirk to evacuate as fast as possible!

As far as who was shooting at them went – well, Emmanuel was right, it COULD have been anyone . . . even their own side.

To start with it could have been German soldiers. The pair of foxes had been causing chaos behind enemy lines for the last two weeks, doing whatever they could to halt the German advance to the coast to capture the town of Dunkirk. This included everything from sabotaging armoured cars and tanks by gnawing through their fuel lines, to scattering food supplies while they slept. They had even sneaked into a German field unit and bitten a general on the bottom when he was making a speech about tactics!

Then there were the British and French soldiers.

3

They might have been on the same side as Charles and Emmanuel, but a fox has to eat, so they *might* have taken a few – just a few! – of their rations (nobody is perfect), which the humans didn't seem to like one bit.

Lastly, and most likely, there was the French farmer whose delicious roast chicken had just disappeared from his kitchen table. With a war on, the animals had agreed a truce to stop eating each other – so cats weren't eating mice, birds weren't eating worms, and foxes weren't eating chickens . . . in theory. But Charles and Emmanuel had been *very* hungry, and since a human had already cooked the chicken, they decided it didn't count!

Anyway, *who* it was really didn't matter; the fact they were *shooting* at the foxes was far more important.

'*Zut alors!* Humans have no gratitude for our work whatsoever,' Emmanuel grumbled as the pair dropped down into the safety of a muddy ditch and the last of the bullets whistled harmlessly overhead.

'Urgh, BLAST, now my paws are all wet! Honestly, we are trying to save these people. If we have to eat a couple of

chickens to survive, what's the big problem? I say, that last one was delicious, wasn't it? Smothered in butter, mmm!' Charles licked his lips.

'If the enemy get their way, there'll be no more chickens for us,' his cousin replied gravely. 'The speed of the mechanical beasts; I've never seen anything like it. So enjoy the lick of your lips, cousin. It might be your last.'

'Nonsense, we just need to regroup, then we'll be back in the fight. Now, we're almost at the beach; let's meet this squad of yours and work out our next move. For the glory of France and all that!'

Sergeant Pierre Elliott of the Royal Norfolk Regiment was tired. He'd fought with his unit for days without rest, his trusty rifle felt like it weighed a tonne and his feet ached as his boots were worn thin.

They were low on ammunition and food, and it had been clear for some time that they were NOT winning the war they had been so eager

to come and fight. The British soldiers were in full retreat alongside their French brothers. For Pierre this was doubly painful as he was half French. His mother, a French doctor, and his father, a British pilot, had met during the First World War and settled in London once it was over. They had begged him not to sign up, but their pleading fell on deaf ears.

If there was a way he could defend both his homelands, he was going to do it. Right now, however, it didn't look like the wisest of choices.

His company had been given orders to retreat, but after a fierce skirmish he'd been separated from the other soldiers and was now lost, trying to make it to the coastal town of Dunkirk. At this current moment, though, he was more worried about being shot at by a French farmer who seemed to have it in for a couple of foxes. Goodness knows why. As Pierre crossed the field, he'd heard the shots boom out and he wasn't going to hang around to ask. '*Ne tire pas!*' he screamed. 'Don't shoot!' Scampering across the muddy field, he looked over to see the two foxes diving down into a ditch, one of them sounding almost as though it was laughing to itself.

I'm glad someone is enjoying themselves! he thought, as he made it to the safety of the hedgerow. *Laughing foxes! I really do need a lie-down and a nice cup of hot sweet tea.*

Charles's earlier confidence disappeared as he and Emmanuel climbed up over the sand dunes at Dunkirk and caught their first glimpse of the tragic scene unfolding on the beach. As far as the eye could see (and foxes have great eyesight) the beach was littered with the signs of a failed military operation. An evacuation was in full swing, with lines and lines of human soldiers queued up, desperately waiting for a space in one of the small rowing boats that were making their way to the Royal Navy ships anchored in the deeper water.

Further up the beach towards the town, Charles could see soldiers destroying the army vehicles so they couldn't fall into enemy hands. It was clear to the young agent that this battle was lost, and if the young men – and animals – didn't get off the beach soon, they would be in very real danger.

He turned to his cousin, who seemed to be frozen in shock. 'Emmanuel, snap out of it.' He clicked his paws, but the French fox sat back on his haunches.

'What's the point, cousin? Look before you. The human armies of Britain and France are no match for the German one. It's chaos! What can we do? We are mere mammals, foxes, *vermin*! The very people we fight for detest us.'

'Well, there's no accounting for taste. Come on, old bean. I'll tell you what we do: we escape, regroup, have a lovely dinner at my favourite spot in Piccadilly, and then we come back to fight again. Now, on your paws, soldier, let's get out of this disaster.'

'But how?' his cousin protested piteously. 'The beach is crawling with humans. We'll never get on board one

of those iron whales!' Emmanuel gestured to the hulking Royal Navy ships.

'Well, that is where we come in, *mon ami*!'

The foxes turned to see a ferret, a badger and a mole emerge from the dunes.

'My friends! Charles, these are the animals from my village I've been telling you about.' The fox sprang to his feet. 'We've been fighting together since the beginning of the invasion.' Seeing his squad seemed to give Emmanuel a new lease of life. 'Corporal Marie Badger and Private Dimitri Mole are our best engineers. And Sergeant Jean Ferret, my second in command, is an expert in sabotage and skulduggery.'

'An animal after my own heart!' Charles said with a smile.

'*Enchanté*.' The ferret shook Charles warmly by the paw.

The squad had scavenged some berries, a slice of pâté, bread, cheese and milk from a local farm. The animals took a couple of minutes to rest and eat as they worked out a plan.

'So what have you learned? Can we make our escape? It looks hopeless,' Charles said ruefully.

'To a lesser company of the French Animal Army, maybe, but to us? Pah.' The ferret smiled, wiping some milk away from his lips. 'But it won't be easy. The poor human troops are surrounded. They have nowhere to go, so they must wait for the small boats to come and get them. It's very dangerous, as they are being attacked by the flying German beasts, and they will capsize in the cold water if too many humans get in a boat at once.'

'That bad?' Emmanuel raised his eyebrows.

'It's awful.' His second in command shook his head sadly. 'But all is not lost; at the far end of the beach is a long narrow pier. It's the only place the large ships can come in close enough to load the troops on without the small boats. You see it?' he asked, passing the foxes a pair of binoculars.

The never-ending sea of khaki-clad soldiers waiting patiently for their salvation stretched from the tip of the pier all the way back to the beach.

'It's jam-packed. There's no way we can get on there

unnoticed!' said Charles.

'With the two best engineer-diggers in the whole of the French Army? *Mon ami*, have some faith.' Dimitri smiled. 'Follow us.'

The squad led the foxes to a small hole in the side of the sand dunes, an entrance to a tunnel covered by bracken and foliage.

'I KNEW you'd been up to something.' Emmanuel smiled proudly at his troop.

'Where does it come out?'

Jean explained. 'Right by the pier. We will make our move in darkness; we climb along the underside of the pier and board the ship as it comes in. I've spoken to the ships' rats and cats from earlier boats as they were docking – good animals, trustworthy – and word has been passed. There's a boat leaving tonight, maybe three a.m. They say it might be the last to sail. If we don't get on it, I don't like our chances.'

Charles looked down the hole, then glanced at the pier in the far distance. It was a long way to travel in a sandy

 13

tunnel, dug in haste, but if the others had been using it already, it had to be safe enough . . .

'We move tonight then. All of you get some rest. I'll take first watch,' Emmanuel ordered.

The squad tucked themselves down among the grasses on the dunes for an uneasy few hours. Charles looked up at the sky and thought of the war to come. If France, which had the biggest army in the world, could fall, what chance did the rest of the world have?

The sound of machine-gun fire woke Charles. He leapt to his feet and scrambled to the top of the sand dunes to join his cousin with the rest of the squad.

A German ME-109 plane – a Messerschmitt – was flying low over the beach, firing on the soldiers below.

Emmanuel looked away, grimacing. 'Cousin, we have no time to lose. Dunkirk will soon fall. Squad, get ready to move – *allez*!'

One by one the animals dropped down the hole. Charles was last to go. The small entrance gave way to a steep drop that he skidded down on his bum, like a slide. Then it levelled off and a long passage stretched into the distance, held up here and there by branches. The whole tunnel system creaked and groaned with the weight of the sand on top of it.

Charles was amazed – it was an incredible feat of engineering. 'Marie, Dimitri, this is unbelievable. How did you do it?'

'We are diggers! It's what we do.' The badger smiled. 'But it was built in haste, and has already been used too many times. I'm not sure how much longer it will hold, so we need to move fast.'

The tunnel was tiny, and even though foxes spend a lot of time underground, Charles felt a little uneasy. This was *nothing* like his charming home beneath Shaftesbury Avenue – it was only just big enough for each animal to squeeze through on all fours, and the only light came from a dim torch Marie the badger held in her mouth at the front of the squad.

After they'd been travelling for some time, they heard a loud drone above: the German Messerschmitt planes were back. The tunnel lay only a few feet below the surface of the beach. Would the animals be safe from the gunfire? All they could do was hold on to each other, as explosions sounded overhead.

Just then, a bullet whipped through the sand above them, narrowly missing Emmanuel's ears. It smashed into one of the branches holding the tunnel up, the structure buckled and the earth started to give way around them.

'MOVE!' Marie shouted. The badger ran as fast as she could, closely followed by the other terrified animals. As Charles looked behind him, he could see sections of the tunnel collapsing as the weight of the sand above crashed down. Ahead, he saw that Marie and Dimitri had quickly dug a makeshift hole to the right. It was tiny, but it was an air pocket that could save their lives.

'Charles, hurry,' his cousin shrieked over the noise. Not daring to look behind, the fox dived for the cover of the air pocket, as everything around him went black.

'I told you we should have dug deeper! Honestly, you badgers, far too hasty. You should always trust a mole for the surest foundations,' Dimitri laughed as Marie batted him playfully on the nose. Shaking sand out of their fur, they turned upwards and slowly started to dig their way to the surface.

Charles shook his head – these animals were extraordinary. They'd been shot at and almost buried alive, but somehow they kept their sense of humour.

Emmanuel checked his watch. 'We must hurry. The boat will be leaving soon.'

'We're almost there,' Dimitri said, just as Marie's paws broke through into the cold night air.

'Wait for a minute while I check the coast is clear,' said the badger, climbing out on to the beach.

Charles breathed deeply in the cool night air, feeling more than a little grateful to have reached the surface.

Marie's face reappeared. 'OK, *mes amis*. Luckily we are close to the base of the pier. It's very dark, and the humans' attention is elsewhere. *Allez*.'

One by one the animals scampered for the relative safety of the long pier. Looking up, Charles could see the hulking silhouette of the giant iron ship that they hoped would be their salvation.

'OK, Jean, what now?' whispered Emmanuel.

'Stanley, the ship's cat, is expecting us. Many animals have been evacuating, so he's no stranger to all this. He'll throw over a rope for us.'

They climbed, gingerly at first, but gradually more sure-footedly, across the criss-cross girders supporting the pier. In no time they were next to the stern of the ship.

'Stanley!' the ferret hissed, and almost immediately a porthole at the bottom of the boat was opened and the smiling face of a tabby cat wearing a Breton cap appeared.

'Jean? Good to see you again, me old china. Blimey, you got enough friends with ya?' He laughed. 'Not to worry, more the merrier. Right, let's get you Frenchies to safety, shall we?' He threw over a rope, which Jean caught and tied to the girder.

'Come on, quickly now. I heard the first mate say we're

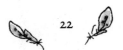

ready to get out of this mess. Hurry!'

'Charles, you go first,' his cousin instructed.

Charles looked down at the inky-black sea below. He'd had a couple of dips in the Thames before, and he didn't fancy ending up in the cold water. Gritting his teeth, he pulled himself up the rope, climbing one paw after the other to the porthole, where Stanley hauled him on board.

'There we go, fella, we'll get your mateys across in a jiffy, then we'll all have a nice cup of cocoa. Hold on a sec . . . Oh no!'

Charles didn't need to ask what the problem was. The engines had started, the shouts of the sailors from up on deck could be heard as they were casting the ropes off, and the ship was moving . . . Looking out the porthole Charles could see his cousin and his band of soldiers looking on helplessly. As the ship had started to pull away from the quayside, the animals' rope had been torn from the pier. Now there was no way the rest of them could get across.

Charles was horrified. He'd vowed to protect his cousin, and now he was deserting him.

'Emmanuel, I'm so sorry! I'll be back, I promise!' Charles screamed above the noise of the engines.

Almost as one, Emmanuel and his squad stood and saluted. 'Go, cousin! We'll meet again soon. I hope . . .'

Charles waved back, watching the pier recede, then slumped down on a sandbag in shock. How could this have happened? He'd abandoned his cousin and his friends to a dangerous and uncertain future. He'd never forgive himself.

Suddenly a faint cry for help snapped him out of his stupor.

24

'Mr Fox, no time to feel sorry for yourself!' Stanley shouted. 'That sounds like a soldier in the water . . . and no human will be able to hear him from the deck.' He dragged Charles to the porthole, where they could make out the outline of a human in trouble.

Pierre was indeed in deep trouble. He'd waited patiently for his chance to board the HMS *Shikari*, bound for the safety of Dover. But as the last of the men was boarding there was a scrum and he was accidentally tipped into the water. Surfacing from the cold sea, he could already see the ship edging away. It seemed like the destroyer was travelling very slowly, but still too fast for him to swim to keep up.

Weighed down by his backpack and his uniform, and having not slept for three nights, he wasn't certain he could even make it back to the shore.

'Help, HELP!' he screamed, but to no avail. He was done for.

Stanley acted quickly. 'Help me lower this rope down; we'll attach it to the beam behind me. He'll be as heavy as anything, but I think the two of us can do it.'

The rope hit the water below with a loud splash. Feeling it go taut, they hoped the poor human had a strong enough hold and started to heave him up.

The rope whacked Pierre in the face as it hit the water, but he didn't care – someone had heard his cries. He grabbed hold of it and tied it around his foot. Slowly but surely he was hauled up by his rescuer.

As he reached the porthole, to his disbelief he saw what looked like a fox and a cat . . . but before he could take in the scene, a pair of enormous hands grabbed him from the deck just above.

'Blimey, where did you come from, mate?' the sailor exclaimed. 'You're lucky I was passing by. Doubly lucky, as they say this will be the last ship out of here. The poor fellas on that beach - doesn't bear thinking about. Now, let's get you safe and warm - this way.'

Pierre gladly followed. He shook his head to clear the bizarre scene he'd clearly imagined from his mind. *A fox and a cat?* He knew that lack of sleep could make you see things that weren't there, but really?

Charles looked out of the porthole to watch the Dunkirk skyline lit up by the explosions of nearby fighting. If you didn't know what they were from, it would almost look beautiful. But how could anything look beautiful now? The world he knew would never be the same again, and what possible difference could he make?

He was done with this war.

3

1943

Bow Street Courts: The Basement Cells

'Wakey-wakey, rise and shine!'

Charles heard a cheery voice and the jangle of keys, and groggily opened one eye to see the cold morning light streaming into his prison cell. At the hatch in the heavy door appeared the smiling face of a bull terrier, with a breakfast tray in his hand.

'Jerry, you are a marvel. Honestly, Mrs Houndstooth is a very lucky lady.'

'Oh, sir, you'll make me blush,' the dog replied, smiling. 'Can't start the day without boiled eggs, buttered

toast and a nice cuppa.'

Charles rolled himself out of bed to take the tray from Jerry. Then he adjusted his silk pyjamas and poured himself a cup of tea.

'It never fails to impress me how you manage to conjure up such a feast every morning.' He slurped at his tea. 'There's a war on! Animals' *and* humans' food is being rationed. I mean, have you tried this awful tinned fish they've started serving for lunch? Even the name is disgusting: Snoek! Bleurgh . . .' Charles paused, before trying to *casually* add, 'I say, you couldn't introduce me to the lovely chicken who provides the eggs, so I could, *err*, thank her personally?'

'Oh, Mr Charles, you are a charmer, but you must think I was born yesterday,' the bull terrier chuckled. 'I don't need to remind you that our wartime truce against eating each other is protected by law. And that, sir, is how you came to be at the pleasure of His Majesty in the first place!'

'Oh well, it was worth a try.' The fox smiled ruefully as he slumped back on his bed, licking his lips.

'Do you mind me asking, sir, why you are still here? You've been locked up for six months now, and every time you have an appeal hearing, you're back down here. I mean, it's nice to have you and I'm glad you've made the place your own,' he said, looking around the cell that looked more like a fashionable London apartment than a prison. 'But with the war on I thought you'd want to do your bit. All you've got to do is promise not to "bother" any more chickens until we've secured peace.'

Charles stared at the ceiling. '*Do my bit . . .*' he muttered to himself.

He'd done his bit and then some, and look where it'd got him. His cousin and his pals were almost certainly dead. Dunkirk had fallen, followed quickly by the whole of France. Now the German army had control over swathes of Europe and the prospect of victory seemed as far away as ever.

What possible difference could the animals, *any* animals, make against the might of the human war machine? The Prime Minister, Bertie Bulldog, made great speeches, and the animal population signed up and helped in their droves, but Charles had seen it first hand and thought the whole thing was hopeless.

As to why he was now languishing in his cell – well, Jerry was right. He loved chicken. Not in a friendly way, more in a way that involved an oven, some potatoes and lashings of gravy. He loved chicken in casserole, stew, soup, salad! You name it, Charles loved chicken in it. So he did what any self-respecting fox would: he ignored the ban and carried on eating chicken. Which involved catching and, err . . .

dispatching them . . . into his belly.

Sadly, the authorities took a dim view of this behaviour, so for the last six months Charles had been behind bars. It wasn't all bad. Jerry was a sweetheart, and anything beat going back to France to learn the true fate of his cousin. So he was perfectly content to wait out the rest of the war locked up.

'I'll consider it carefully, Jerry, but right now I'll have my post-breakfast nap,' he said as he climbed back into bed.

'Ah, not today, Mr Charles. I've been given strict orders to get you ready to travel. So best clothes on, if you please.'

'Me? Where to, old thing?' the fox asked, confused.

'Beats me, sir, but they were very insistent.'

All too soon, Charles was being released from his cell and taken down a corridor to two big blue doors. Standing by them were a pair of beagles in plain clothes, waiting for him.

'Morning, gents. Lovely day for a stroll. You boys here to chase me over some fields?'

One of the dogs looked at the other and shook his head

in frustration. 'They said he'd be like this, Harry. Don't rise to it.'

He turned to face Charles and spoke in a low, authoritative tone. 'Mr Charles Redfearn, we have orders from the highest authority in the land to transport you to a secret location but we need your assurance this conversation will be kept under wraps.'

'Of course.' Charles could see they weren't kidding.

'Right then, time for some extra precautions,' the chief beagle said cheerily, and his partner quickly tied a thick blindfold over Charles's eyes.

As he was frogmarched out of the prison, Charles couldn't help but wonder where in the world they could be heading. And what did they want with him? These beagles looked official, but he was a washed-up secret agent. After Dunkirk he'd lost his taste for the whole thing, and there was no way he was going back.

The dimly lit, low-ceilinged room that appeared as his blindfold was removed gave little clue as to where Charles

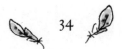

now found himself. He took a seat opposite a mahogany desk, behind which were various maps of occupied Europe and the coastline of the south of England. To his left was a long, red leather chesterfield sofa.

'You can leave us now,' an authoritative voice commanded the beagles from behind Charles.

He turned to see a tall ginger cat in an impeccable grey pinstriped suit walking through the door. 'Morning, Charles. Care for a glass of milk?' he said with a smile as the dogs left the room.

'Best fill it up to the top; the poor chap will be needing it,' added a gruff-toned voice from the shadows to his left. Charles turned again and gulped.

The cat was Charles's old boss and friend, the head of the secret service, Sir Claudius Browne, but the other voice was none other than the animal Prime Minister, Bertie Bulldog himself! Which could only mean one thing: Charles must be directly below 10 Downing Street. This was the beating heart of the animal government, the most important address in the country.

'Erm, I'm not entirely sure why I'm here, but I can assure you I promise not to attack any chickens again . . . until the end of the war,' said Charles, quite confused and, if he was honest with himself, a tiny bit scared of the powerful pair.

'We'll get on to that,' chuckled the cat, enjoying his discomfort. 'It's good to see you again, old thing. Now, I know you know who I am, and our esteemed guest will need no introduction, but do you have any idea what we want from you? And no, it has nothing to do with your appetite.'

'None whatsoever, sir.'

'Oh, put the poor fox out of his misery,' Bertie piped up. 'You're playing with him like a mouse.'

The cat came to sit opposite Charles on the corner of the desk.

'Very well. Charles, you were one of the finest agents of your class, but since you've been, ahem, *otherwise* engaged, we have been very busy. The secret service has agents all over France and mainland Europe, helping the unwitting humans to try and disrupt the German war machine. We've done great things. Moles, badgers, foxes, cats, dogs, birds, all working together to wreak havoc. Digging up railway tracks; gnawing our way through telephone cables; disabling cars, tanks and planes. We've risked our lives, and many of our agents have paid a terrible price.'

Charles's mind strayed to Emmanuel and his team – it would be a miracle if they were still alive.

'And now we think – *think* – one of our team might have found a most important document that could help the Allies win the war: the German army's defence plans for the whole Atlantic coastline. But there's a problem, which is where you come in. The document he has discovered is locked away in a French chateau, and it's encrypted. We need someone to break in, decipher it, make a note of its contents and return it without the German humans being any the wiser.'

Charles looked at both of his superiors, baffled. 'Sir, firstly, I'm not an agent any more. I currently live in jail! And don't you have the Ninja cats to do this sort of thing?'

he said, referring to the ancient order of cats who made up the most elite wing of the secret service.

'All of them are on missions elsewhere. No, Charles, it has to be you,' Sir Claudius replied.

'But I don't know how to decipher any codes,' said Charles, knowing he was running out of reasons.

'We've thought of that, don't worry. We have a master codebreaker from the team at Bletchley Park. We just need someone to get her to the chateau, make sure she stays safe and then get her out as quickly as possible. And the best, most qualified animal for the job is you.'

'Sir, with respect, I don't want any part of this war. And you wouldn't either if you'd seen what I did in Dunkirk. The human German army is too powerful, and frankly too terrifying, for any animal to do anything about it. Plus, even if I did agree, I'm not sure I'm sharp or fit enough. I've been out of the game for—'

'Your country and all animalkind are asking you to do your duty,' the Prime Minister interrupted solemnly. 'Sir Claudius says you're the best agent we have.'

'Of course, no one can make you go,' added Sir Claudius. 'But there's one more thing you should know: the agent who discovered the document, and sent us the intelligence, has since disappeared. Charles, it's your cousin Emmanuel.'

Charles was stunned, speechless. He slumped back into his chair, his mind whirring. Emmanuel was still alive? How could that be? Somehow his cousin had made it through the last three years of carnage and chaos, and now he'd uncovered a document that could change the face of the war. That was all he needed to know. If Emmanuel was still out there, Charles was going to find him.

He drained his glass and looked back up at his two superiors, who, seeing his steely gaze, could tell he'd made his decision. 'I'll be needing another one of these milks, sir. When do we fly?'

'I knew you'd come to your senses, Charles. Good show and thank you.' The cat smiled appreciably, moving towards a side door. 'Now, how about you meet your partner? Charles, allow me to introduce

Miss Gertrude Featherhorn.'

He opened the door to reveal a brown, prim, cardigan-wearing and haughty-looking . . . CHICKEN.

4

As quick as a flash, Charles bolted over the table and made a lunge for her. He wasn't in control of himself; his fox instinct had taken over. As far as he was concerned, she was food and he was ready to eat. He was just about to reach his prey when he found himself flat on the floor with the powerful frame of Sir Claudius standing over him. Charles struggled to get up, but it was no use; the strong cat had him pinned to the floor.

'You do *know* I'm a Ninja, old thing,' the cat chuckled. 'And is that any way to greet your new partner?'

'I say, Claudius, are you sure about this?' Bertie Bulldog piped up, slowly getting off the sofa as if he was heading for a Sunday-morning stroll. 'We can't very well have your

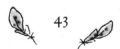

agents ripping each other limb from limb.'

'It's quite all right, sir,' answered the cat, staring at Charles. 'I'm sure it won't take long for Charles to realise that if he wants to see his cousin again, and rescue him from whatever peril he is in, his only chance is to trust Miss Featherhorn and work with her as a team. Isn't that so, Charles?'

 44

Charles knew his boss was right; somehow he'd have to fight his urges and not attack Miss Featherhorn. This chicken was – and he couldn't quite believe he was saying this – his *partner*! He nodded his head in defeat.

'Well, if you're quite sure . . .' the bulldog said, as much to himself as anyone else. 'Miss Featherhorn, Charles, Sir Claudius, best of luck on this endeavour – the fate of the war is in your hands. I pray I won't regret this decision.'

He gathered his walking stick, put on his top hat and left, closing the door behind him.

'Let's try that again, shall we?' Sir Claudius smiled, releasing Charles from his grip.

Charles got to his feet and dusted himself down.

'Look, sir,' he sighed. 'I'm sure Miss Featherhorn is great at codes, but aren't there any other—'

'We've considered every option, Charles. We would send her alone, but there are some things she simply can't do, which is where you come in.'

'Such as?' asked Charles, with a feeling of dread creeping over him.

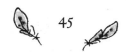

45

'Ahem, well,' Gertrude interjected. 'Firstly, it's nice to meet you, Mr Redfearn. I'm sure even after that . . . *unconventional* start, we'll enjoy working together. You should know that I have a fear of flying and heights in general. I get seasick. I have to get eight hours' sleep minimum, or I can't decipher a thing. And I'm allergic to hazelnuts, pineapple . . . and eggs.'

'But you're a chicken! How in the world can you be allergic to eggs?'

'That's an interesting story, which I—'

Sir Claudius interrupted with a clap of his paws. 'Gertrude is a genius codebreaker, the best we have, fluent in five languages and an expert in self-defence – well, sort of . . .'

'What does that mean?' the fox asked, exasperated.

'It means I'm a pacifist. I don't like fighting, so I generally just try to flutter out of the way,' she answered, head held high.

Charles sat down with his head in his paws, groaning.

'Come on, Charles, I think you two will make a crackerjack team. Now, there's no time to waste. A car is leaving in five

minutes to take a human secret agent to Tangled Wood Airfield for his flight tonight, and you are hitching a ride all the way to occupied France.

'As soon as the plane lands, get out of there and make for the farm two miles south. The local Resistance will meet you there, and properly brief you. We'll arrange getting you back to England with them, so you don't need to worry about that. Really, the mission is simple: find Emmanuel, get to the chateau, retrieve the plans, Miss Featherhorn cracks the code, and you both get back here safe and sound without the Germans knowing a thing about it. Silence and speed are the key.'

Sir Claudius rose to look at the unlikely pair. 'Like the PM said: the fate of the war could well be in your hands. Good luck.' He saluted, and the fox and chicken uncertainly returned the salute. The door was opened, and the two beagles reappeared to usher the pair upstairs.

The heavily camouflaged car rumbled along the country lanes towards Tangled Wood Airfield on the Kent coast.

Charles and Gertrude had sneaked into the boot as the car was waiting for the human secret agent to leave his briefing, and they'd been travelling for a couple of hours so far.

His new partner had been asleep under a blanket since they left London. Charles didn't mind – it gave him an opportunity to take stock of what had been a crazy couple of hours. To be honest, he was dumbfounded. This morning he'd have gladly eaten this chicken on the spot . . . without salt. Then he was told she was one of the most important animals of the whole war, whose life he had to preserve at all costs, and working with her was the only way to help his cousin. The mission sounded like it had little hope of success but he had to believe he could complete it if there was even the tiniest chance of finding Emmanuel. He'd do what he had to, even if it meant babysitting a chicken.

From his seat in the car, Pierre was gazing out at the English countryside. Not that he could see anything - since the blackout began four years before, all

the streetlights had been turned off, and people had put up special curtains to block any light coming out of their houses.

Pierre couldn't quite believe how his life had turned out. After escaping Dunkirk, he'd qualified as a Commando and excelled. Then the approach had been made from Colonel Maurice Buckmaster to join the Special Operations Executive (SOE) and be a secret agent in the field. He would go back to France to 'set Europe ablaze', as Churchill had put it. Pierre had jumped at the chance.

Being half French, he cared deeply for the country and its people. And now this was it; finally his chance to go back and help them prepare for their liberation.

He was elated but he was also terrified, and uncertain of what lay ahead.

The jolt of the car pulling to a stop on uneven ground woke Charles from a deep slumber. On the other side of the boot Gertrude was still fast asleep, making a strange chirp-like snore.

She's not even awake and she's annoying me already, he thought. Looking out of the crack in the boot of the car Charles could see a few bushes nearby, and he could hear a lot of commotion outside.

'Psst, PSST!' he hissed at the chicken. 'We're here, wake up!'

'I'm quite awake, thank you very much, and have been for some time! I've just been resting my eyes.'

'Well, that's just a lie. I heard you snor— Oh, never

mind. Look, I'm going to pick the lock of the boot, then we have to get to the bushes without the humans seeing us. Ready? Three . . . two . . . one!'

Charles pushed the flapping chicken out of the now open boot, and followed her as she scampered to the cover of the bushes.

'Could you not ruffle your feathers so loudly? Do that in France and we won't last a day,' an annoyed Charles whispered.

'I was NOT ruffling my feathers, but even if I was, a little more support from you would not go amiss. You might have forgotten that I'm very nervous of flying and the last thing I need is you making me more anxious.'

'I'll tell you what makes *me* anxious: babysitting a chicken who has NO IDEA what she's getting herself into. We are about to land in enemy-occupied France; we'll be lucky if you're not on someone's plate within twelve hours – and trust me, the French know how to cook chicken! I've agreed to take part in this mission for one reason only: to save my cousin. If we're going to survive, you need to do *exactly* what I say, *exactly* when I say it. Are we clear?'

Charles was quite pleased with this speech, but Gertrude's attention seemed to have drifted. He followed her gaze to two birds who had emerged from the undergrowth and were watching the arguing couple with confusion.

'Charles and Gertrude?' a small bird asked, as much to break the tension as anything else.

'Yes,' the pair answered a little sheepishly.

'Welcome to Tangled Wood Airfield. Good to meet you both. I'm Wing Commander Linus the swift. Follow me.'

5

Charles had heard of Linus and his exploits in the Battle of Britain. Most of the animal world had. This small bird had, together with his comrades, helped win the conflict which had given both humans and animals hope that they could somehow win the war. He couldn't help but feel a little embarrassed as they followed Linus through the undergrowth.

'Sorry about that. We're just getting to know each other. New partners generally have a few teething problems here and there,' Charles tried to explain.

'Don't worry.' Linus smiled. 'It's none of my business. I'm on strict instructions to get you aboard this flight without any humans seeing you, and to NOT ask any questions. I have to admit, seeing a chicken and a fox teaming up does look a little odd. But my best friend is a peregrine falcon, so I know a fair bit about odd pairings. Here we are,' he said, as they came to the edge of the undergrowth that bordered the human airfield. 'There's your ride.'

Ahead of them was a fixed-wing plane with landing gear shaped almost like a pair of slippers. It looked old and slow. Its engine was starting to rumble.

'I'm not getting in that!' Gertrude said, with a wobble in her voice. 'It doesn't look at all suitable for flying in.'

Charles winced. 'Do you see any other aircraft lined up?'

54

'It's quite all right,' Linus reassured Gertrude, patting her gently on the wing. 'It's a common reaction to seeing the old Westland Lysander. It's hardly a Spitfire, but trust me, when you've got to land in a small field with barely any room, you'll be grateful for those lovely wheels. And if this war has taught us anything, it's to not judge a book by its cover. Now, let me make sure it's safe to board. Tyrone?'

'On it, chief.' The white-faced barn owl saluted, then silently took off and swooped over to the tail of the plane. They could just make out his silhouette as he twisted his neck almost all the way around, to scout the whole airfield.

'Urgh, always weirds me out that owls can do that,' Linus laughed.

The owl hooted an ear-piercing screech. 'And that,' the swift added.

'Right, Miss Featherhorn, you're up first. Get over to the tail of the plane. There's a small compartment where Tyrone will help you get stowed.'

Gertrude clucked and fluttered her way over to the owl, and clambered reluctantly on board. Charles

shook his head despairingly.

'Try not to give her too much of a hard time.' Linus smiled. 'She might be an unconventional partner, but she volunteered for this and that shows bravery. The one thing I've learned since I've been flying is that if you don't work as a team, you stand no chance. Now, it's your turn. Good luck – I hope your mission goes well.'

The swift shook the fox by the paw then watched as Charles ran over to the plane and jumped in. Tyrone closed the hatch behind him and flew back to his squadron leader.

Within minutes, the human pilot and his quarry, the young SOE agent, had climbed on board and the squat little plane taxied out to begin take-off. Linus and Tyrone watched as it faded into the night sky.

'Well, they are a rare old pair,' Tyrone observed. 'Be a miracle if we see them again. All that fighting and bickering! They won't last five minutes.'

'I hear you, old friend. But I hope you're wrong. From what I'm led to believe, all our fates depend on them.'

*

The Westland Lysander was, as Linus had said, a marvellous plane for getting agents and equipment in and out of occupied France. It had excellent short landing and take-off capabilities, which meant the pilots of the 'Special Duties' squadron could land pretty much anywhere, from small, improvised airstrips to flat fields. It was a marvel. All of this detail was lost on Gertrude and Charles, however. Gertrude spent the flight with her head hidden behind her wings, and Charles – who had never actually been on a plane before – found the rumbling a little bit nerve-wracking himself. (Not that he'd ever admit it.)

As they flew across the English Channel, he looked over at Gertrude and felt a twinge of guilt and shame. The words of Linus rang in his ears: *If you don't work as a team, you stand no chance*. The little bird was right. Gertrude might make a better lunch than a secret agent, but they were partners and there was no point adding to their difficulties by being mean to her. For better or for worse, they were stuck with each other.

'It's OK, you know, to be frightened,' Charles shouted over the noise of the engine. She clucked a little bit, but didn't reply.

'But these things are very safe, so long as no one is shooting at you, which, admittedly, I can't guarantee won't happen. In fact, it probably will . . . OK, look, all I'm saying is, don't worry *too* much, and I'm sorry . . .' He swallowed the last bit of the sentence hurriedly.

Gertrude peeked out from behind her feathers. 'Beg pardon, I didn't quite catch that?'

'I said, these things are very safe!' Charles said slowly and loudly, as he started to blush.

'No, I got that part,' she replied, clearly enjoying every second of his discomfort.

'I'm SORRY!' Charles almost yelled. 'Look, I get it, you're a genius. And I need to make allowances for the fact that you're not a trained agent. I'm just used to someone a little more—'

'Foxy?' Gertrude asked with a smile. 'Trust me, I'd much prefer to be putting my brain to good use, rather than all this mindless bravado. And don't go thinking you're some great catch either. It's not my choice to be buddied up with someone who may very well have eaten my cousin. But one has to prioritise one's duty in wartime, so I'm prepared to wipe the slate clean and start from scratch.'

She stuck out a wing, which Charles met with his paw. 'Right, well, err, thanks for being so understanding.'

They felt the plane starting to descend and Charles crouched to peer out through a small crack in the door. As the Lysander slowly dropped through the clouds, he could see torches on a landing strip below, guiding the plane down.

'We'd better get ready,' he shouted. 'When we hit the ground, we need to be prepared to run to the nearest hedgerow. I don't fancy any human spotting us, and if any German soldiers heard the plane there could be a nasty welcoming committee for the poor human upstairs. You and I don't want to be caught in the crossfire.'

Gertrude nodded seriously. He could tell she was scared, but resolute.

As soon as the plane landed, Charles sprang into action, opening the door and jumping out. He could hear the pilot and the passenger unclipping and getting ready to disembark too.

'Quickly,' he whispered, reaching a paw up to help Gertrude down to the ground. 'The passenger will be getting off from the ladder side, which means we run to those bushes on the right. Three . . . two . . . one . . . go!'

He raced as fast as he could to the undergrowth. Any second he expected to hear the crack of a rifle ring out, but just as his lungs were bursting, he made it to the safety of the bushes.

Breathing heavily, he looked back. The Lysander's engines were still running and he could see the SOE agent walking around the plane in his direction. Charles sensed movement to his left, and heard a branch snap on the ground. He turned, expecting to see Gertrude, but instead there was a human – a German soldier! Who was raising his rifle at the young British agent.

Before he'd worked out what to do, a flash of brown feathers flew past him, as Gertrude launched herself at the young soldier. Bewildered and confused, the German didn't know whether to run or fight. He shooed the bird away, steadied himself and made to aim at the agent once more. But just as he was about to squeeze the trigger, a set of teeth dug into his arm. He howled in pain as the rifle fired.

Pierre heard the rifle crack from the treeline and immediately hit the ground. He fully expected

62

a volley of gunfire to follow, but instead there was a wail from the bushes, almost like someone was being attacked. Whatever it was, he wasn't hanging around to find out. Bolting towards the plane for cover, he turned his head briefly to see if he could spot the origin of the shot, but all he could see was what looked like a chicken being chased by a fox.

'What on earth?' He shook his head, and screamed to the pilot, 'Get yourself out of here!'

'Taking off already,' came the reply.

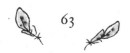

Running as fast as he could towards the other side of the field, he saw movement up ahead. 'Blast, I'm done for,' he muttered. But just as he was about to put his hands up he heard a call in French from the bushes.

'*Mon ami*, the code is POULET! *Allez*, quickly, follow me.'

It was the sweetest sound he'd ever heard. He saw the faint outline of a young French woman beckoning him, and he sprinted towards her – and safety.

The young German stared down at his bloodied arm. Had he just been bitten by a fox? And attacked by a chicken? He looked up to see the plane taking off, and no sign of the SOE agent. *Curses. What will I tell my commanding officer?* he thought. *I might just keep this incident to myself.*

After running a good distance away from the airfield, Charles and Gertrude paused to catch their breath.

64

'Gertrude,' Charles panted. 'That was unconventional . . . but brilliant! Where did you learn that move?'

'I did tell you I could put my fluttering to good use. And you're not the only one who's had training, Mr Redfearn. The chicken coop can be a pretty brutal place to grow up. Luckily, I studied under an Onagadori – a rare breed of chicken that has honed the art of poultry self-defence. He taught me everything I know. It's just that I'd rather not use it.'

Charles shook his head in wonder. There was more to this chicken than met the eye.

A loud bark suddenly shattered the peace of the quiet woods.

'Cripes, we've got company. We need to get moving – and fast!' Charles sniffed the air and caught the clear whiff of more than one dog.

'Mr Redfearn, I think we can take on a dog or two.' Having had a taste of action, Gertrude was wide-eyed with adrenalin.

'Steady on,' replied Charles. 'It's one thing surprising a young soldier; it's quite another taking on dogs who are trained to rip us limb from limb!'

'Come on, Charles, there's no way I can outrun them – we must face the danger head on. I have a plan. You'll need to do the fighting. I *am* a pacifist after all, but trust me.'

'Very well,' said Charles, rubbing his ear with a paw. How quickly the roles of chicken and fox had been completely turned on their head!

Two German attack dogs dashed through the trees, picking up the scent of the saboteurs, barking as they went. They would catch up with this fox in no time. His scent grew so strong that they knew they were nearly upon him, when they almost ran into a chicken. She was lying across their path, wings outstretched, crying loudly.

'Oh, *messieurs*,' she wailed in a strong French accent. 'My saviours, thank you so much for coming to my rescue. I was just going about my chickenly business when a beast of a fox grabbed me and was dragging me back to his den, when he was startled by your barks. He left me for dead and ran off that way.' She pointed behind her.

The dogs stared at her, then at each other, then back at her. Should they believe her or attack her? Unluckily for them, the decision was taken out of their hands . . .

'TIIIMBERRR!' came the cry, as Charles swung in on a low-hanging branch, deftly connecting a sharp kick to one of the dogs, who in turn went crashing into his companion.

The blow knocked both of them out cold.

'That was brilliant. Well done, Charles,' said Gertrude, applauding.

'Never mind me, where did that piece of acting come from?' asked Charles, dusting himself down.

'Oh, stop it, you flatter me. Though I was in the Chichester Poultry Amateur Dramatics Society before the war, and they said my Titania was worthy of five stars,' she said bashfully.

'I'll have to come and take in a show when this is all over. Now, let's get moving before these two lummoxes wake up. It'll be dawn in a few hours, and we need to get to our rendezvous point to meet the Resistance.'

6

There were still a few hours of darkness left when the pair arrived at their rendezvous point: a farm on the edge of the woods. All was still and quiet, both animals and farmers fast asleep. There was no sign of the Resistance squad and, looking over at Gertrude, Charles knew she was almost done in and needed some rest. He wasn't faring much better.

'Let's scout for a safe place to sleep,' he said, placing a gentle paw on her wing.

There were two huge barns, but the doors were bolted shut. The pigs in the sty were not entertaining any notion of a fox and a chicken sharing their quarters. The yard felt too exposed.

'There is one option, but I'm not entirely sure you'll like it,' Gertrude said, steering Charles round the back of the farmhouse.

'You have to be kidding me,' Charles said. 'A chicken coop? Have you lost your mind? Gertrude, less than twenty-four hours ago I very nearly succeeded in eating you.'

'But look at us now: best of pals. So I'm sure you can keep your foxy appetite under control for one night.'

Charles was so exhausted he didn't have the strength to argue. 'We'd better hope I don't wake up hungry.'

'We'll make a vegetarian of you yet. You'd best stay out here for a minute – this might be a slightly difficult sell. Bear with me.'

Gertrude disappeared into the coop, and all Charles could hear was a good deal of unhappy clucking. She reappeared a few moments later.

'They're very nervous. Luckily, chickens worldwide are big fans of our royal family, so if anyone asks, you're a distant cousin of King Georgie the corgi. Best behaviour now, Charles – I'm trusting you. Mind your head on the way in.'

Charles entered the arched wooden chicken coop (although he did bang his head . . . 'Oww!'). Inside was a scene that, given his recent history, should have been paradise. It was wall-to-wall hens, all sitting on their straw nests in different compartments, and all of whom were staring at him with a mixture of fear and curiosity.

'This is the gentlemen I told you about, ladies. He's a great advocate for chickens' rights, has been a herbivore for a good five years now and I'm sure you can see the corgi bloodline in the shape of those lovely ears. Isn't that right, Charles?' Gertrude smiled.

'Err, well, quite. Good evening, ladies, *enchanté*,' he said uncertainly. 'I realise this might be a slightly odd situation, but trust me, I just need to rest up for a few hours and I'll be out of your feathers. Not that I'll be in your feathers at all, if you catch my drift.'

Gertrude led Charles to a quiet compartment in a corner of the coop, where he collapsed into the hay and fell immediately into a deep slumber.

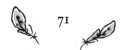

*

He woke with a start as a cockerel crowed outside. *Best keep my head down. I don't imagine he'd be too happy to see me strolling out of here*, Charles thought to himself.

He gazed up at the coop ceiling and tried hard to ignore the rumbling in his belly. 'Chickens are not food,' he muttered under his breath. 'Chickens are not food, chickens are not— But maybe just one teeny-tiny egg? NO! I can't. I mustn't. But could I?'

In twenty-four hours Charles had gone from being in prison for 'stealing' chickens, to protecting, respecting and even *befriending* one. He knew he had to keep his urges at bay. He closed his eyes but all he could see was roast chicken and omelettes and . . . *That was it!* Omelettes were Emmanuel's speciality. Every time he wanted to eat a chicken, he would try to conjure up his cousin's face instead to stay focused on the mission at hand. His heart panged. The thought of failing to finding Emmanuel was more than Charles could bear.

The creaking coop door raised him from his stupor.

 73

They weren't alone. If the dogs had tracked them down, or the farmer was up and about, there was nowhere to run to. He cursed himself. He had been exhausted, but how could he have been so stupid to agree to being so boxed in? With no alternative, he curled up into a ball and made himself as small as he could. In the compartment next to him, he could sense Gertrude was stirring, but he had no way to alert her to the danger without revealing himself. A shadowy figure got closer and closer to their compartments. It was no use, they were trapped. Charles took a deep breath and got ready to fight for their lives.

A small brown face suddenly appeared out of the gloom. '*Mon ami*, I did NOT expect to find you snoozing among such feathery company! Can I bring you some breakfast?'

'Jean!' Charles leapt to his feet and embraced his old ferret friend. 'You're alive! After Dunkirk, I feared the worst.'

'Such little faith! It would take more than a few planes and tanks to suppress the Resistance. Dimitri and Marie are with me as well.'

74

Gertrude poked her beak out from her compartment to greet Jean. '*Bonjour*,' she said with a yawn.

'I'm sorry, where are my manners? Jean, this is Miss Gertrude Featherhorn, my partner on this mission and our master codebreaker.'

Jean looked at the chicken, then Charles, in disbelief before quickly composing himself. '*Mademoiselle*, a pleasure,' he said graciously. 'Any friend of Charles's is a friend of ours. France thanks you. Charles, you are a changed fox!'

'Trust me, I don't recognise myself either. Now, what news of Emmanuel?'

'The last we heard he was alive and being held in a chateau not far from here. But our intelligence is patchy at best.'

'So what exactly happened?' asked Gertrude.

'We had heard of a top-secret meeting taking place in the chateau. A family of mice who live in the walls are loyal to the Resistance and they've been our eyes and ears. Emmanuel broke into the chateau, where he found encrypted documents on the desk of the human general.

But before he had a chance to make his escape, he was caught in the act. I believe it was the same general whose bottom you both bit back in 1940 in Dunkirk, and he still has it in for foxes. The last we heard from the mice, the plans were under lock and key in a safe and Emmanuel was to be skinned to make a fox stole for the general's wife. We don't *believe* that has happened yet, but we have no time to lose!'

The ferret was interrupted by the human farmer flinging open the door to collect his morning eggs. He stared in shock at the fox *and* ferret in his chicken coop. For a moment there was silence, then he screamed in rage. The chickens clucked and fluttered into the air in fright, and all was chaos. Wiping a stray feather from his face, the farmer ran down the coop waving a dangerous-looking rake but just as he hurled it in the direction of Charles, Jean and Gertrude (who, understandably, later remarked that it was a tad unfair being lumped in with a fox and a ferret) he slipped in chicken poo ('NOT MINE,' insisted Gertrude) and they managed to escape.

'That was a little dicey,' panted Charles when the three had stopped running. 'Thanks, Gertrude.'

'I already told you it *wasn't* mine. Oh, never mind.' She smiled, realising the fox was joking.

'I don't think it's going to get any easier where we're headed, *mon ami*,' Jean said. 'Come. Dimitri and Marie will meet us on the way.'

As the ferret led them through the countryside, the muddy fields became steeper and steeper until they finally reached the top of a hill that looked down into a deep valley. Dimitri and Marie were waiting for them with warm smiles, warm hugs and, to Charles's delight, warm croissants and mugs of hot chocolate. They passed Charles a pair of binoculars, while Gertrude took the opportunity to lie on the ground with her feet in the air ('For my circulation, naturally,' she clucked). Charles could see a wide river, and on the other side of the valley, built into the hill, was an imposing-looking chateau. The only way in seemed to be via a long, winding lane that led from their side of the valley across a rickety bridge and then back up through the chateau gates. Stone walls loomed high on all sides of the building and grounds.

'Blast, that's no good. Any way we can tunnel in?' he asked the engineers.

'Alas, no, the basement walls and floors are made of stone.' Marie sighed.

'We can't very well make our way along the lane and just

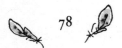

78

knock on the door. How on earth did Emmanuel get inside?'

The ferret smiled. 'What's your climbing game like, *mon ami*?'

'I spent one summer scaling Mont Blanc, but I haven't climbed seriously for a long time.'

'Well, this is about as serious as it gets.'

'Ahem, there is one small problem with this plan,' said Gertrude, getting back to her feet and waggling her wings for effect. 'I can't climb at *all*.'

'We have to get you in there somehow. If you can't decipher the secret plans the whole mission is a waste of time – and Sir Claudius gave us strict instructions not to remove them from the chateau,' Charles said in exasperation.

As Charles and the members of the Resistance debated the benefits of a home-made catapult to launch Gertrude over the walls, versus using a local buzzard to drop her in (which they eventually discounted on the basis that Henri really could *not* be trusted and might fly off to feed the master codebreaker to his hungry chicks), Gertrude's attention was distracted by a slow-moving vehicle trundling along the lane leading to the chateau.

'If you'll allow me,' she said, grabbing the binoculars. 'Aha! A horse and cart.' Charles could see a plan was hatching. 'I think I might have an idea,' she said with a wry smile.

*

'Are you out of your mind?' Charles asked, as Marie strapped supplies across Gertrude's feathery chest. 'This is a terrible idea.'

'I need to get into the castle, and we're all agreed that there are no other sensible options. The wagon was clearly carrying supplies for the kitchen, so I simply wait for another, then jump on board. It's foolproof.'

'But if the wagons are heading for the kitchen, full of ingredients for dinner, then the humans will think *you're* an ingredient for dinner!' Charles couldn't decide whether she was stupid or courageous.

'Charles, I thank you for your concern, but you must have a little faith in my skills. I've got us this far, haven't I?'

Charles had to admit that she was shaping up to be a rather better secret agent than he'd imagined. Not that he would say that out loud . . .

Dimitri rolled out a map of the chateau and they all leaned in close.

'When you get to the kitchen, try and sneak out immediately,' Charles said fiercely. 'DO NOT draw

attention to yourself. After Jean and I free Emmanuel from this tower we'll make for the library – it should be the quietest, least busy place. Meet us there. Together, we'll work out where the general's safe is and as soon as you've read the code, we'll escape.'

'Just one more thing,' Jean said with a sad smile. 'We have heard from the mice that the chef in the chateau, Monsieur Scoffer, loves cooking coq au vin. So don't be his next course, *mademoiselle*.'

'That's really helpful,' Gertrude said sarcastically. 'I'll bear it in mind.'

7

From her hiding place in a bush by the side of the road, Gertrude waited for her chance. A few official-looking cars sped by, one with a distressed-looking general in the back, and she almost got run over when a troop carrier whizzed past. But just as she was thinking her plan was never going to work, a horse and cart came into view, its contents covered by a thick canvas tarpaulin.

'Bingo,' she clucked quietly to herself.

Not being able to fly properly came with its limitations, and even though the cart was plodding slowly along the dirt road, for Gertrude it felt like a high-octane chase. Running as fast as her drumsticks would carry her, she came up alongside the cart, then, leaping for her life, took

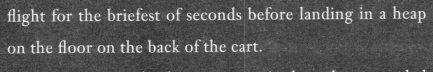

flight for the briefest of seconds before landing in a heap on the floor on the back of the cart.

Once on board, she was surprised to hear startled clucking from beneath the tarpaulin. She peeked beneath to see . . . CHICKENS! It couldn't have been more perfect. Who would notice one more chicken in a cart of hundreds? What a stroke of luck.

'Don't mind me, ladies,' she clucked in perfect French. 'Just joining the party.'

The French hens didn't know what to make of the strange newcomer.

'Are you here to lay for the soufflé tonight?' a confused poulet de Bresse called Céline enquired.

'Err, indeed. I heard they were after eggs of the highest quality, and what an honour it would be to work with Chef Scoffer. Please don't tell anyone that I'm not from your farm – I'm just desperate for the opportunity.'

Céline smiled. 'Come sit with me, child. I will tell you all about the soufflés my eggs have been used for.'

Gertrude settled down for the remainder of the bumpy ride. All was going to plan.

But as the cart passed through the arched stone entrance of the chateau and the imposing wooden doors closed with a bang behind them, Gertrude had a terrible feeling of dread. Had she pecked off more than she could chew?

*

Charles lowered his binoculars and shook his head with a combination of admiration and bemusement from his hiding place alongside the chateau's great stone walls. Gertrude had certainly come a long way from the scared little chicken he'd first met. He and the rest of the troop had made their way quietly through the undergrowth, crossed the river on the underside of the bridge to remain safely out of sight, and were now preparing for the last part of their journey: the terrible climb. Charles hadn't really dared to imagine his cousin was still alive all these years, but he was now fearful about what they might find inside. Were they in time to save him?

Jean grasped his paw and whispered, 'He is strong, your cousin. Trust me, he'll be OK. Come, let us go and make sure he doesn't end up around someone's neck.'

Marie and Dimitri secured ropes to a nearby tree and acted as the support team. Charles and Jean began the steep climb to the turret high up above, where they believed Emmanuel was being kept.

Jean climbed like he had a rocket strapped to his back

88

and was soon out of sight, but for the fox it was incredibly hard going. He hadn't really done any exercise while he'd been locked up, and now he regretted all those delicious naps he'd taken. Every muscle in his body ached with pure exhaustion as he slowly dragged himself to the top window of the turret. He pulled himself over the sill and flopped down on the cold stone floor.

'Jean,' he puffed. 'I had no idea you, or any ferret, could climb like that!'

Jean didn't answer.

'Jean?' Charles sat up and peered into the gloom.

There was no sign of the ferret.

Instead, Charles found himself face to face with two enormous dogs guarding a wooden door.

'*Qui êtes vous?*' they growled menacingly, and began to approach him.

'Ah, wrong side of the tower,' Charles cursed to himself under his breath. He was just casting a nervous glance about him for an escape route that *wasn't* jumping straight back out of the window, when he heard a familiar French voice approaching from the stairs below.

'*Messieurs, messieurs*, you have been working hard for these stupid humans, and, tut tut, they never show you any appreciation, so the kitchen wanted to send up these bones with their compliments. After all, it's not every day you save so many chickens from a pesky fox, *non?*'

Charles turned in amazement to see Jean, wearing a waiter's apron and carrying a tray of bones under a cloche. Jean winked at Charles and gestured to the bones.

The dogs were already drooling at the delicious smell.

'We do work very hard. *Merci, monsieur,*' one of the dogs said, and greedily went to grab the tasty bones.

'*Une minute*, comrade.' The other dog looked confused. 'If we're here guarding the fox . . . what is THAT fox doing here?'

'NOW!' shouted Jean, and in a flash the fox and ferret had grabbed the bones from the metal tray and bonked each guard dog over the head, leaving them both incapacitated.

'That was inspired, Jean!' Charles clapped his friend on the shoulder.

'*Oui*, I had a lot of time to think what to do when I was waiting for you to climb up the tower,' Jean said with a chuckle as he bent down to check the pockets of the dogs' uniforms. He handed Charles a set of keys.

The fox put them to the lock with a shaking paw and threw open the door to his cousin's cell.

There, lying slumped in a corner, was Emmanuel's limp body. Charles looked back at Jean, who hung his head in despair. They'd come all this way . . . but they were too late.

A thin voice broke the silence. 'I can't believe you wasted good bones on those two idiots. I bet there was some perfectly good meat left on them.' Emmanuel smiled weakly as he turned to face his rescuers and opened his eyes. 'I knew you'd come, cousin.'

Deep in the bowels of the chateau, Gertrude was beginning to think she'd made a big mistake. As soon as the chickens had been unloaded, they'd been shoved roughly into a

cage in the corner of the kitchen. It had quickly become apparent (at least to *her*) that they were not there to help with a soufflé . . . She had to think of something, and fast.

Monsieur Scoffer, the burly French chef, was practically dancing around the kitchen in excitement as he began to prepare the general's supper. 'Coq au vin is a thing of beauty,' he was muttering to himself. 'All the ingredients are perfectly in sync with each other. The mushrooms, the bacon, the shallots, and all held together by the juiciest, tenderest, *freshest* chicken . . .'

'Anyone else hear that? *Anyone?*' asked Gertrude, but the other hens paid no attention and kept clucking on about how marvellous it was that their eggs were being used in the famous soufflé.

'This is doing nothing for our PR,' she muttered to herself, at a loss about what to do. Then the door opened and a stressed young orderly hurried into the kitchen.

'Monsieur Scoffer,' he addressed the chef nervously.

'*Non!*' the chef replied, clearly frazzled. 'I am about to create a work of art and I gave strict instructions not to be disturbed.'

'Right, well, I'm sorry,' the nervous soldier answered, 'but I was told to tell you . . . the coq au vin . . . is to go!'

'What? WHAT?' he screamed in the young man's face. 'Monsieur Allain Scoffer does not do food "TO GO"!'

'Please don't blame me,' the orderly begged. 'I've just been told that the general, the regiment and the whole contents of his office are to be transported by train back to Germany tonight. And that means his dinner needs to be . . . to go.'

'Urgh, very well. It will be ready in an hour or so.' He turned and advanced on the chickens' cage with a gleam in his eye. 'I'll just have to *speed up* the process.'

Cripes! thought Gertrude. Turning to her fellow chickens she spoke quickly. 'Ladies, we are in deep trouble. If we don't do anything right now, we are very soon going to be smothered in bacon and mushrooms, which, while I'm sure would be a great honour for some of you, is not my idea of fun. So when Monsieur Scoffer opens this crate we have to make a run for it. Who's with me?' she cried. The cage was silent. Thirty confused chickens just stared back at her. Unfortunately, she didn't get time to think what to do next, as a huge hand reached into the cage and grabbed her.

'I always like to cook the noisy ones first,' the chef proclaimed as he carried Gertrude towards the cooker.

Gertrude knew she was done for. Pacifist or not, this was a time for direct action. Summoning all her strength she wriggled out of the chef's grip enough to give him a sharp peck on the hand.

'Oww!' The chef dropped Gertrude and she fluttered down to the ground. 'You pesky *poulet*!' He went to chase after her, but he slipped on the greasy floor and went careering into a shelf of eggs, sending the entire thing crashing to the ground.

The whole crate of hens gasped in horror.

Céline the old hen piped up first. 'Gertrude was right. He's planning to put us in that pot.' She turned to her fellow chickens. 'And, ladies, no one messes with our eggs. *Vive le soufflé! Vive le poulet!* And *vive la Résistance!*'

As one, the chickens roared in rage and burst out of the cage.

Gertrude looked on in delight and Monsieur Scoffer in horror as pots, pans and food all went flying, mostly aimed at the chef. He took shelter under a kitchen table, and the hens ran amok.

One aimed a potato at the chef, but missed, instead hitting an oil lantern, which promptly shattered and started a small fire that began to spread across the table.

Sensing her chance, Gertrude made for the door.

'Thank you, *mon amie*!' she shouted to Céline. 'Will you be OK?'

'Don't worry about us, we'll be out of here *tout de suite*,' she smiled as she waved a wing. 'We just have to teach Monsieur "Breaky Eggs" a quick lesson.'

The chef howled in pain as a group of chickens pecked at him. He fled from under the table and out of the back door, the chickens flapping in hot pursuit.

Leaving the chaos behind, Gertrude checked the coast was clear and made her way quickly down the corridor. Now all she had to do was find Charles, crack the code and get the vital information home to help win the war.

8

Pierre couldn't believe where he had found himself.

Sophie, the young Resistance agent who'd found him in the field, had taken him to a local farmhouse to meet the head of the *réseau* (local Resistance fighters). But almost as soon as they arrived, the farmhouse had been encircled by German troops. Had somebody trailed him and Sophie? Or had they been betrayed another way?

All of them - except Sophie, who *somehow* managed to slip away - had been captured. Now they were being transported to a grand chateau, almost certainly to be questioned by the dreaded

German police: the Gestapo.

Looking out of the back of the truck, he cursed his luck. He felt like he'd let his country and his family down. He HAD to escape. There was no way he was going to spend the rest of the war as a prisoner - he needed to be part of the action! He held a glimmer of hope that Sophie would find a way to save them. But as the truck approached the huge wooden doors of the chateau, that possibility seemed less and less likely.

Pierre's attention was drawn to a scene unfolding at the side of the chateau. A chef was running as fast as he could, pursued by a flock of angry-looking chickens. Pierre barely had time to think how odd this was (even with all the other strange things that had happened to him of late) before a deafening alarm sounded, and chaos broke loose.

Charles, Emmanuel and Jean descended from the tower and made their way to the library. They had to hide whenever human sentries approached, but they kept to the shadows and soon found the entrance: a pair of huge oak doors. Charles put a paw to the door and—

NEEEEEOOOWNEEEEEOOOWNEEEEEOOOW

'What is that infernal din?' Charles shouted, grimacing at the horrible noise. 'Whatever it is, it could work to our advantage if the castle is distracted – it might be a perfect cover for us. Now, Jean, are you sure this is the place?'

'Of course, the dormice confirmed it. The library doubles

up as the general's study; the safe is behind the painting on the wall. Where is this codebreaker of yours?'

'Gentlemen.' Gertrude poked her head out from behind the library door. 'I've been waiting here for *ages*. What kept you?'

Charles flung his arms around her. 'Thank goodness you're safe! Gertrude, this is my cousin Emmanuel.'

Gertrude went to shake the fox's paw. He was almost frozen in shock – his own cousin embracing . . . a *chicken*?

'*Enchanté*,' Emmanuel whispered in disbelief.

'Charles, we need to hurry. I overheard they are shipping everything out of here tonight,' Gertrude said, all business.

'Pick your jaw up off the ground, Emmanuel,' Charles said with a chuckle. 'We've got a safe to crack! By the way, Gertrude, is that alarm anything to do with you?'

'Let's just say you might not want to go into the kitchen for a while.'

'Who *are* you, Miss Featherhorn?' Charles said, as they crept into the library.

The room ahead of them had an impossibly high ceiling

and a mezzanine level that stretched all the way around, with a ladder on wheels. It was filled from floor to ceiling with books, apart from a huge fireplace, over which hung a massive oil painting of a fox hunt.

'You've got to be kidding me,' said Charles, looking up at the painting. 'These guys are just asking for it.'

The foxes and the ferret lifted the painting but the weight of the picture was too much, and it went crashing to the floor.

'Oops,' Emmanuel said sarcastically. Luckily the noise of the alarm obscured any attention the smash would have otherwise drawn.

Charles surveyed the safe. It had a huge dial in the centre, with a ring of numbers round the edge.

'Can you crack it?' asked Gertrude.

'Piece of cake.' Charles smiled. 'I've been doing these since the thirties – this should be easy!'

He put his ear to the door and spun the dial one way then the other several times. Soon enough they heard the welcome clunk of the lock falling open.

'Crackerjack!' he congratulated himself. 'Right, Miss Featherhorn, over to— Oh, *blast*.'

The safe was empty. They were too late.

For a few seconds, no one said anything. Charles, Jean and Emmanuel all looked defeated, but Gertrude wasn't having any of it.

'Come on, chaps, the race isn't run yet,' she chirped. 'We've all come so far! Charles, a day ago you were in prison, dreaming of roast chicken – and now you're back on top secret-agent form. Emmanuel, you were almost made into a scarf, but now you're free. Jean, you organised this whole rescue. And I . . . *I* set the chateau on fire!'

'You did what?' exclaimed Charles.

'Never mind. Listen, we know the plans are being transported somewhere tonight – there must be something in the general's study to give us a clue where to. Let's get searching.'

'She's right.' Emmanuel smiled. 'The *mademoiselle* speaks the truth. I can't believe I'm taking lessons from a chicken, but we must not give up now.'

Charles nodded wearily, but before they could do anything more, a door in the far corner swung open.

'Quick, under the table,' Charles ordered. The team ducked beneath a grand desk under a large window in the corner of the room.

'We have to hurry, sir,' a human voice said urgently.

'Yes, yes,' the general answered impatiently, sitting down at his desk, his feet coming dangerously close to Jean's nose. 'Is the coq au vin ready?'

'I believe Monsieur Scoffer, ahem, is having some difficulty, sir . . .' he answered apologetically.

'Blithering idiot!' the general erupted.

'Sorry, do you mean him or me?' the orderly asked.

'BOTH OF YOU! How hard is it to make a simple chicken dinner? Now, are the documents securely packed? Those plans need to get back to Berlin pronto. The security here is a joke. I still can't believe a fox – a fox! – was found in this study. Honestly, if my own idiot guards can't even keep the wildlife out, what chance have we got against our enemies? Still, that fox should be a beautiful

fur stole for my wife by now.'

'Err, about that, sir, we think the fox might have got away. Sorry.'

'It was in a cell in the tower – how on earth could it possibly have escaped?!' The general shook his head in dismay. 'And when will that infernal alarm stop?'

'Once again, apologies, sir. There's a bit of a fire in the kitchen and the men are trying to get it under control. It seems the hens for your coq au vin escaped as well . . .'

This was too much for the general to bear. His face reddened as he screamed at his subordinate. 'At least tell me the British spy is still under lock and key . . . or did he escape when someone tried to make steak *frites*?'

'We still have him, sir. Will you be questioning him tonight?'

'Sadly not. He'll have to come back with us to Berlin. Make sure he's escorted *securely* to the train.'

Under the desk, Charles turned to his friends and whispered, 'We HAVE to get on that train, Gertrude. Somehow we need to find those plans *and* try to free this poor agent. Jean, any idea where this train will be leaving from?'

'*Oui*, the only station is a few miles away. We'll have to hurry to make it, but I have an idea.'

'Righto, as soon as this general shifts his feet, let's move as quickly and quietly as possible. Emmanuel . . . Emmanuel?'

The French fox seemed to be in a complete daze as he listened intently to the general.

'Cousin, you hear this general? I swear I know his voice from somewhere.'

'Emmanuel, I really don't think this is the time.'

'I've got it – just before Dunkirk! It's the general whose bottom we bit! What a coincidence that it's the very same man who would have made me into a scarf. I can't let this go unpunished.'

'Please, cousin, we need to leave. Don't do what I think you're going to do.'

But Charles's pleas fell on deaf ears. Emmanuel smiled mischievously and whispered, 'This is for us, Charles, for Mademoiselle Gertrude, for the Resistance . . . and

for the glory of France!'

He jumped out from under the desk and
bit the general right on the
bottom – *again*!

The general howled in shock and pain and leapt into the
air.

'FOX!!! Another fox! Get it!'

He and the orderly pulled out their pistols and fired at the escaping party. But by the time they'd got their shots off, the animals had reached the door and the bullets pinged harmlessly off the doorframe.

'That was intense, my friends,' Emmanuel squealed. 'I'm sorry, but I couldn't resist. And you have to admit: it was priceless.'

'I loved every second of it. You are far more fun than your cousin!' Gertrude said giddily.

'I'm not sure who's worse,' said Charles, shaking his head. 'Jean, whatever your plan is, lead the way pronto.'

The ferret grinned and took them to some steep, stone spiral stairs.

'Up? Why are we going up?' asked Gertrude, confused.

'Well, it helps if you're going to *fly*!' the ferret answered.

9

'You have to be out of your mind,' said Charles, as the team raced up the stairs. 'You want to entrust her safety to a buzzard who has no allegiance to the Resistance and who you already admitted might take her home to meet his hungry chicks . . . and not in a good way!'

'*Mon ami,* if we want to make this train, it's our only chance. Plus, look at you: a day ago you two were at each other's throats, and now you're best friends. I'm sure she can charm Henri.'

'He's right, Charles,' piped up Gertrude. 'We have to risk it – the mission is too important.'

'Spoken like a true member of the Resistance. *Et voilà,* here we are.' Jean opened a small door that led to the

 III

ramparts at the top of the chateau.

Charles looked down to the inner courtyard to see a hive of activity. There were cars, trucks, motorbikes and even a few tanks, with hundreds of soldiers and staff readying for departure.

'We don't have much time,' Charles said. 'If we're going to do this, let's do it now.'

The small ferret climbed up a turret and, cupping his paw, made an almighty screech.

For a minute or two, they all looked into the still night and saw nothing but darkness. But then, just as their hope was fading, they saw several enormous wings come into view, nothing more than shadows against the dark sky. As they got closer, Charles saw the shape of four giant birds. They circled the chateau once, then landed on the rampart by the group.

'*Bonsoir*,' Jean said timidly. 'It's good to see you, Henri.'

The giant bird looked at the group with contempt and, to Gertrude's alarm, like he was sizing up his next dinner . . .

'Jean,' he said finally. 'What on earth are you doing using the animal emergency call? I was ready for my bed and now my friends and I are dragged out of our nests for what? A ferret, two mangy-looking foxes and, I have to admit, a *tasty*-looking chicken.'

'Who are you calling mangy!' Charles bristled as he stepped towards the giant bird. Jean moved quickly to defuse the situation.

'Henri and friends, thank you for getting out of your nests to help. I promise you, this *is* an emergency. Look below you: the Germans are leaving for Berlin by train. On that train are secret documents, vital for the war effort. These two agents have been tasked with uncovering them, and we humbly ask you, the most powerful, wise and important bird in the whole of the valley, to help us in this quest.'

The buzzard said nothing for a minute while he inspected his talons. Henri was a proud, vain bird who cared little for other animals unless he was eating them. Would Jean's compliments convince him?

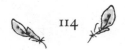

'Nice try, ferret, but no dice. Why should I care what the Germans do? They've been here for four years and my life has not changed one bit. If anything, it's got better because there are fewer human hunters in the fields, which means more food for me. I really don't care about anything else. But now you've woken me and my friends and so I'm afraid you'll have to pay a price for the inconvenience. Let's see, a ferret, two foxes and a chicken – not a bad haul. Shall we, boys?' The birds displayed their talons and closed in on the gang.

'This is going well,' sighed Emmanuel.

'Sorry, boss, looks like we'll go down swinging,' Jean replied with a grimace.

'WAIT JUST ONE MINUTE!' All eyes turned to Gertrude as her screech cut through the night air.

She composed herself before saying, 'Mr Buzzard, while I fully understand that this war hasn't had the least effect on you or your family, that is not the case for most of us in the animal community. Yes, you could eat us, tear us limb from limb and feed us to your families . . .'

'Too much!' whispered an alarmed Charles.

'But,' she continued, 'what would that achieve? Momentary happiness? Perhaps. Indigestion from such a varied dinner, and all that mangy fur? Definitely.'

'She's right there,' piped up one of the buzzards, gesturing to another. 'Poor Claude, had it terribly last week after he ate that duck, frog and mouse platter, *oh la la*.'

A sorry-for-himself Claude nodded, confirming the story.

'Surely the better thing to do,' Gertrude said with raw emotion in her voice, 'is to think what you can do for your fellow birds, mammals, amphibians. This is a fight we're all in together, for the glory of France!'

For a moment no one said anything; all eyes were trained on the chief buzzard.

'WE SHALL FEAST . . .' he suddenly shrieked, and everyone – buzzards included – gasped as one. '. . . ON THESE SILLY MEN AND THEIR MACHINES! FOR THE GLORY OF FRANCE AND OF ALL BIRDKIND! COME, MADEMOISELLE CHICKEN, WE WILL

HELP. JUMP ON, *ALLEZ*.'

'*Mon Dieu*, she's only gone and done it,' said Jean with relief.

Climbing on to the backs of the giant bird and his friends, they took off into the night sky.

'How are you back there, little chicken? Are you scared?' Henri said to Gertrude as they soared through the air.

'Quite the contrary,' hollered a surprised Gertrude. 'I'm actually having the time of my life. Wheeeeeeee!'

'You're by far the most fun chicken I've ever eat— I mean *met*,' the buzzard quickly corrected himself.

'Err, thanks, I guess!'

The squadron soared over the treetops of a forest, their route lit by a full moon. Pretty soon the trees began to clear and ahead there were fields lying in a broad valley. They could see smoke from the stack of the engine, and then the train came into view.

*

Pierre had no idea where he was heading. Among the other prisoners on the train there was nervous talk about them being transported to Germany for further questioning.

He looked glumly out of the window. Silhouetted against the moon he saw four huge birds, seemingly racing to keep pace with the train, though why on earth would they be doing that? He shook his head to clear the thought. He envied them their freedom. How long until he, too, would be free again?

'Blast, it's left the station. We've missed it,' lamented Charles.

'No matter, you're flying with the finest France has to offer. Just get ready to jump,' said Henri.

On his command, all four birds banked steeply, so they were flying directly over the train, matching its speed.

'*Trois, deux, un!*' Henri squawked, and all four animals leapt at the same time to land safely on the roof.

'*Bonne chance,*' said the buzzards as they wheeled away. Charles saluted them, then gathered his team for a huddle.

'OK, the most important thing is to find the carriage the documents are in, then after Gertrude works her magic we'll try to help the British human agent. Jean, I'm counting on you to come up with an escape plan.'

They started at the back of the train and, carriage by carriage, Emmanuel and Charles held Gertrude and Jean by their legs so they could spy through each window. They saw soldiers playing cards, a beautiful restaurant car where the officers were enjoying a sumptuous dinner, and even the general having a bath to ease his sore bottom (which made Emmanuel almost fall over with fits of laughter), but nothing that looked like the location of the plans. Until they got to the last-but-one carriage.

'There's a solitary soldier holding tight on to a big briefcase, and two very stern-looking dogs,' Gertrude said as Charles pulled her back up to the roof. 'We need to get them out – but how?'

'Gertrude, please don't overthink it. They're dogs, and what do dogs like to chase?' Charles winked at her.

A knock at the door startled the snoozing German soldier. He had been told not to let this case out of his sight, but it was such a boring duty. There was nothing to do, plus he was *starving*. They'd said someone would be

along with some food, but that was ages ago. This must be his dinner.

'About time, Karl,' he said with a sigh as he opened the door. But there was no Karl. The soldier looked left and right, confused, then between his legs appeared a . . . fox?

Before he had time to react, the two dogs had almost knocked him down in their eagerness to chase the animal. The fox disappeared into the next carriage with the dogs hot on its heels, and the door swung shut behind them. While the soldier pondered what to do, there was a flash of red fur and he suddenly found himself tumbling from the train on to the muddy bank below. He rolled to a stop, his head spinning. Had he *really* just been kicked off a train by a fox?

From the roof of the train Jean leaned over and gave Emmanuel a thumbs up, then looked back at the chicken.

'The coast is clear, Mademoiselle Gertrude. We have to go and help Charles, so over to you.'

Gertrude flapped down into the carriage and went to work. The case was on a desk so she drew up a chair

and opened it to reveal a big brown folder, bound with red string. She pecked until it came undone then started to go through the pages. All they contained were reams and reams of numbers. To all but the most advanced of codebreakers, it would read as gibberish. And, if Gertrude was honest with herself, for a few minutes it felt hopeless. The stress of the last couple of days was catching up with her; she felt exhausted and was struggling to focus. From the carriage next door she could hear a huge commotion – it must be the fight between her friends and the dogs. She wiped the sweat from her eyes.

'Oh dear, I hope they are OK. Focus, Gertrude!'

Taking a deep breath, she tried to remember her training. Slowly at first, but then with more ease, the figures started to take shape and she was able to decipher the code. Her eyes flicked over the pages and in no time she had both cracked and memorised the entire contents of the document. In her head she now had the whole plan for the German army's Atlantic defences. She was the most important chicken, animal, even human in the whole of the

war effort right now. She needed to get back to London –
and fast.

Shutting the case and leaving it exactly where she'd found
it, Gertrude stepped gingerly out of the carriage. The next
car along was silent now, and she feared the worst. If her
friends had been captured – or *worse* – how on earth would
she get back to London? She slowly slid back the door and
braced herself.

Charles, Emmanuel, Jean and the two dogs were all

sitting round a small table . . . playing cards! Charles was in the middle of telling a story.

'And I said to the wing commander, if your human is *that* stupid, they didn't deserve the parachute to open!'

The dogs found this hilarious, and they fell about laughing.

'Oh, Charles, that is brilliant. It sounds like your humans are as silly as ours.'

'Ahem,' interrupted Gertrude.

'Gertrude! Chaps, this is the chicken I was telling you about. Gertrude, meet Henrick and Per.'

'But why aren't you fighting?' Gertrude asked in disbelief.

'Oh, we had a bit of a dust-up, but then we kind of started chatting and it turns out we have a lot in common.'

'*Ja*, we all enjoy badminton and knitting,' said Per enthusiastically.

Gertrude raised her eyebrows – she couldn't imagine Charles with knitting needles. He put a paw to his lips to stop her from saying anything, before continuing:

'Exactly. Plus, their humans work them too hard and don't feed them enough, so Jean and Emmanuel said they'd get them some top-notch French grub, and maybe even find some friendly farmers to adopt them. And in exchange, they're going to help us get off this train.'

'Gosh,' exclaimed Gertrude. 'I certainly wasn't expecting that!'

'It's the least we can do,' smiled Henrick with a toothy grin.

'So what's the plan?' she asked.

Before Charles could answer, they heard the most almighty bang and their world turned upside down. The train flipped over, sending the animals flying. Everything went black.

10

It was Charles who was the first to come to. In a daze he rolled over, coughing. He checked his comrades, and to his relief they, too, started to stir. The windows of the upended train had all been blown out, so he helped get his team to their feet and they crawled out of the wrecked carriage.

The scene outside was chaotic: all the carriages had been derailed, there was fire everywhere, and most of the German soldiers were walking in a dazed shock.

It was pitch black, but in the light from the fire Charles spotted several figures darting to and from a carriage deliberately, like they weren't shocked that the train had been derailed. Almost as if they'd planned it.

'Who are they?' he asked.

Emmanuel's smile was one bursting with pride – he knew exactly who'd derailed the train. 'That's the Maquis, cousin – *la Résistance*.'

Pierre didn't know which way was up. He had seen the flash before he heard the bang. Sensing something was going to happen, he was partly ready for the crash and held on to a luggage rack. But when the train was upended, he was still sent flying.

Luckily his fall wasn't too bad and he was on his feet in no time. Should he leave the relative safety of the carriage? If the German soldiers saw him, surely he'd be shot on sight. The decision was made for him when he saw a familiar face poking her head through the blown-out window.

'Sophie!' he said with relief. 'You blew the tracks? How did you know I was on board?'

'We've been tracking you since you were captured! Quickly now, with me.'

Pierre needed no encouragement and scrambled out of the window to follow the young Maquis. The other prisoners were dashing here and there, and the Germans had no idea what was happening.

Ahead, he saw a small truck with its engine running.

'Hurry, it will take you to the plane to get you back to England.' Pierre couldn't believe his luck and ran as fast as he could.

'We need to get on that truck,' said Jean. 'The Resistance have derailed this train to save that young agent so they will have planned an escape route for him. That's your ticket out of here.'

The team raced across the open ground towards the truck, but the German soldiers were starting to realise what had happened and the general was barking orders. He was even more furious than normal.

Shots rang out as gunfire was exchanged between the Resistance and the German soldiers. The animals had to

duck not to get caught in the crossfire.

The truck was beginning to pull away by the time Charles reached it and jumped on the back. 'Run! Faster!' he yelled at his squad. Both Jean and Emmanuel made it, but Gertrude had fallen behind. The German soldiers were catching up with her, still firing at the truck, and a pack of snarling dogs ran alongside them.

'Go!' the brave chicken cried. 'Leave me!'

Charles was at a loss. He wasn't sure he could save her, but he couldn't leave her to be torn to shreds by the dogs or trampled by a dozen soldiers. They'd been through too much together – he'd come so far, *she'd* come so far, and they were so close to getting home. What's more, he'd actually grown to care for Miss Gertrude Featherhorn – she was a friend. There was no way he was going to let her down.

He dived off the speeding truck and ran as fast as he could towards the exhausted chicken. 'Charles, you fool!' she shouted.

'We started this together and there's no way I'm going

131

to let you end up on some general's plate! Climb on board.'

He picked Gertrude up with his teeth and practically threw her on to his back. He ran faster than he'd ever run before towards the back of the truck. Behind them, he could sense the pack of dogs hot on their heels. With all the strength he could muster, he paused to grab Gertrude from his back and flung her towards the speeding truck. She flew through the air for what felt like an eternity. It

didn't look like she was going make it to safety but, just as Charles felt certain she was going to land short, she spread her wings. For the briefest moment she flew – or, to be more accurate, *glided* – through the night air. If Charles didn't know her, he could have mistaken her for a graceful owl or a majestic eagle.

'Can't fly indeed,' he said to himself, in awe of his friend. Then she landed in a tumble, knocking Jean and Emmanuel right over.

Charles had a moment of satisfaction watching his friends speed to safety, before he felt hot dog breath on the back of his neck. He shut his eyes and waited for the end ... and waited ... and waited.

Opening his eyes cautiously, he found himself faced with two goofy grins. Behind the shape of the enormous hounds, the rest of the dog pack seemed to be running in the opposite direction.

'Per, Henrick! How did you—'

'It took us a while, but we explained to them about the badminton, and the knitting, and the French farmers just waiting for a dog of their own to love. Jean and Emmanuel are going to have quite a job on their hands finding new homes for all of us!' Per laughed.

'Now, I believe you've got a plane to catch and a chicken to get home,' Henrick said with a smile. '*Viel Glück,* Charles.'

Charles saluted, then turned and sprinted with all the strength he had left to catch up with his friends.

As the truck turned into the nearby town, Gertrude looked glumly down the road, hoping more than anything for Charles to magically appear. She knew that she was close to safety, but at what cost? Her friend had sacrificed himself for her, and she'd have to live with that forever. In spite of all the good she knew the decoded plans would do, she cursed her decision to ever leave Bletchley.

Emmanuel put a gentle paw on her wing. 'Don't beat yourself up, little *poulet*. It was my cousin's choice. I'll miss him terribly, but he was a brave fox and we should all be proud. I know your heart is breaking and mine is too. I can't believe we'll never see that bushy red tail again—'

'I wouldn't be so sure of that,' interrupted Jean. 'Look!'

Tearing around the corner of the street, Charles sprinted towards the truck. Luckily, now the truck was passing through the narrow streets of the town it had slowed down enough for the exhausted fox to catch up. Emmanuel stuck out a paw and hoisted his cousin up. For a minute, all the animals embraced.

'Cousin, how in the world did you make it out of there?' Emmanuel asked.

'Let's just say German shepherds get a bad rap. You must follow through on that promise of yours, fellows. And I think I'll look them up after the war and send them a gift. Perhaps a lovely package of roast chick—' Gertrude looked aghast. 'Sorry, sorry! Force of habit.'

Charles stopped at the sound of roaring engines. Around the corner came the terrifying sight of motorbikes, *Kübelwagens*, a troop carrier and a small Panzer tank. There was no way they were letting the humans of the Resistance get away that easily.

'We have to do something!' cried Emmanuel.

From inside the truck, Pierre could see the German troops closing in. He looked across at Sophie, who just shook her head.

Pierre's luck had finally run out.

Then, from the corner of his eye, Pierre saw the strangest sight. Was that a flock of chickens driving a jeep?

'Céline!' Gertrude yelled in disbelief as a van drove out of a side road up ahead and swerved past, travelling at speed towards their pursuers.

The old hen waved with one wing as she steered with the other.

'We've been keeping tabs on you, my little chickadee! Never underestimate the power of the *oeuf*!' she cackled.

Gertrude didn't stop to wonder how these unlikely warriors had managed to be in the right place at the right time. All that was important was that they *were*.

Céline turned to her brood of chickens. '*Mademoiselles*, time to repay a favour. Release the eggs!'

The old chicken turned the steering wheel hard to the left and executed a perfect handbrake turn. The back doors of the van burst open right in front of the German vehicles.

The chickens did what she ordered and threw egg after egg. With their windscreens – and in some cases their faces – covered in yolk, the frustrated German soldiers had no idea who was attacking them but were forced to slow to a stop. The general could be heard yelling at his troops once more, but all the soldiers looked so confused by what had happened that none of them were following his instructions.

Gertrude waved in gratitude at the French hens and turned to her comrades, who were staring in disbelief. 'Chickens saved the day again, chaps, don't forget that,' she said with a smug grin.

Pierre and Sophie couldn't believe what they'd just seen. One minute they'd been done for, the next there were eggs everywhere. Had they really just been saved by . . . chickens? In that moment, Pierre vowed to become a vegetarian.

They soon approached a field where the trusty Lysander was touching down. Pierre turned to his

comrade. He wasn't sure what to say.

'Merci,' he whispered, then added, 'Your animals here really are quite odd, aren't they?'

Epilogue

Piccadilly Circus, London

7 June 1944

Tucked beneath the human tea house known as Lyons was Charles's favourite place for a light supper in the whole of London. The jolly café was packed, but he spotted his friend already seated at Charles's regular table. The owner, Gerard (who, to Gertrude's surprise, WAS an actual lion, who had escaped from a travelling zoo in the thirties), smiled and nodded from across the room, indicating he'd take their order in a moment.

Quite a few heads turned when they saw a fox joining a chicken for dinner, but neither Gertrude nor Charles cared.

'Well?' Gertrude asked.

'It's early days, but so far it looks like the invasion has been a success.'

Gertrude breathed a sigh of relief. The day before had been D-Day, when the Allied forces (human *and* animal) had landed in France to try and liberate the country, and then the whole of Europe. If it was successful, it was surely the beginning of the end of the war.

'You DO realise how important the document you deciphered is, don't you?' said Charles. 'We knew the German defences and could plan our invasion accordingly. You've saved thousands of lives.'

Gertrude blushed before asking, 'What are your plans now?'

'I leave tomorrow, to hook up with Emmanuel and his team and make for Paris to help organise the animal Resistance there. The war is a long way from being over. How about you?'

'Like you said, the war isn't finished yet. There's important work still to do at Bletchley.'

'Right,' said Charles hesitantly, 'about that . . .
I was hoping I might persuade you to . . . come with us?'

'What?' Gertrude spluttered as she almost spat her drink
out. 'Leave the safety of my office to go haring around
Europe with you, after I barely made it out last time?
Have you gone mad?'

Charles arched an eyebrow, his offer hanging in the air.

Gertrude placed her cup down and stood up.

'When do we leave?' she said with a smile.

Just then Gerard appeared at their table. 'The usual, Charles?' he enquired.

'Not today.' Charles smiled back at Gertrude. 'We'll take two salads, and can we get them to go?'

Author's Note

Though this book isn't inspired by one historical event, or one specific service in the armed forces, I wanted to highlight the invaluable contribution to the Second World War of three organisations.

Charles's (and Pierre's) story was inspired by the Special Operations Executive (SOE), a British organisation formed in 1940 to carry out espionage, sabotage and reconnaissance to aid local resistance movements.

The character of Gertrude was inspired by the incredible Bletchley Park codebreakers. This group of clever minds worked from a grand estate in Buckinghamshire, and their work to uncover the secret communications is thought to have shortened the war by two to four years.

The inspiration for Emmanuel came, of course, from the French Resistance, a collection of groups that fought the Nazi occupation.

Finally, I'd like to make a special mention of the little talked about Royal Air Force Special Duties Service. This was a secret air service created to provide air transport to support resistance groups by bringing in special agents, wireless operators and supplies.

This book is dedicated in gratitude to all of them.

If you would like to find out more about these amazing humans as well as the animals who supported the war effort, just turn the page!

Want to know more about the Second World War?

In *Spy Fox and Agent Feathers* we meet humans and animals who are trying to help win the war for the Allies – which was a group of countries fighting against Nazi Germany and the other Axis Powers during the Second World War (1939-1945).

ANIMALS DURING THE WAR

The animals in Dermot's story are incredibly brave – and he was inspired by lots of real-life animals who helped humans during the Second World War!

You can probably guess how important cats and dogs were . . . Cats, like Stanley in this book, were often kept onboard ships to help keep mice and rats away from stores of food. They also took on this job in army barracks and other places that were used to store important supplies.

Dogs had lots of jobs during the war. Rescue dogs helped to find survivors after bombs were dropped, and some were even trained to carry medical supplies to soldiers in the field. Some dogs were used to keep watch for the approach of enemy troops, while others were trained to transport messages or to use their sense of smell to find land mines.

There were also more unusual animals that played a role. Elephants were used in Africa and India to help with transportation and heavy lifting. Camels carried soldiers in countries such as Egypt. And in India and Burma, soldiers used mongoose to keep them safe from venomous snakes!

Do you have any pets that have special skills that would be useful during an emergency?

DUNKIRK

Charles and Emmanuel's story starts in a place called Dunkirk – a port town in France. A huge evacuation took place here of British, Belgian and French soldiers, which took nine whole days in 1940. The soldiers needed to leave France because Nazi Germany had invaded. There were about 340,000 soldiers who needed to get on boats from the beach – can you imagine that number of humans in one place? That's almost four times as many people as can fit into Wembley Stadium!

The British had to borrow lots of small boats from civilians (people who were not in the army) as well as their own military ships in order to move them all – some were crewed by Royal Navy officers, but others were sailed by volunteers such as fishermen. This group has become known as the Little Ships of Dunkirk.

THE SOE

In Dermot's story, one of the human characters is Sergeant Pierre Braithwaite. He joins the Special Operations Executive (SOE) and is sent on a mission to France. This secret British organisation was set up in 1940 to help local resistance movements in countries including Albania, Belgium, France, Greece, Italy and Yugoslavia. British spies usually travelled to these places by plane, just like Pierre, but lots of them had to use a parachute to land!

SOE agents often needed to communicate information back to Britain. They sometimes did this with radios that had been designed for this job. First, they would put their message into a secret code – this is called encryption. Then, they would use their radio to transmit the message via Morse code – a special alphabet made up of taps called 'dots' and 'dashes'. Morse code is still in use today, though much less often than during the Second World War, as we now have so many digital ways to communicate.

THE RESISTANCE

France was occupied by the Nazis during the Second World War. The French Resistance was made up of ordinary men and women who worked in secret to fight against the Nazi occupation. They transmitted information to the

Allies, helped Allied soldiers and airmen to escape if they were trapped behind enemy lines, published underground newspapers and undertook missions to sabotage transport and communication. It was very dangerous to be a part of the Resistance and members had to live a secret double life in order to avoid arrest.

BLETCHLEY PARK CODEBREAKERS

During the war, both sides used codes to send secret messages around the world containing vital plans and intelligence. In Britain, Bletchley Park housed the Government Code and Cypher School, where some of the cleverest mathematicians worked together to break the codes used by the Axis Powers.

Some of the work they carried out involved cracking the code created by the Enigma machine – which was used by the Germans for lots of top-secret information. The codebreakers had to create special machines to help them work out this incredibly complicated code, a bit like a very early computer!

In 1939, at the beginning of the Second World War, there were about 150 people working for Bletchley Park. By the end of the war there were more like 10,000. Men and women, members of the armed forces and civilians, all worked around the clock to try and stop the war as soon as possible.

Acknowledgements

My thanks, as always, have to start with my Butch and Sundance at Hachette. Kate Agar and Alison Padley. Both as charming and daring as Charles, as clever as Gertrude, and as brave as Emmanuel . . . where DO I get my ideas . . . I'd be lost without them.

To Ruth and the whole family at Hachette, with a special shout out to Lucy and Jasmin.

To my friend and master of ink Claire Powell. Who never ceases to wow me with how she brings every single character to life.

My thanks as always to James Holland, for his WW2 expertise and guidance.

To all at John Noel Management. John, Jadeen, Darcey and Lucy, for their LONG-suffering patience, and helping me find time to do all the lovely things I'm lucky enough to do.

And to Dee and Kasper, both for editorial and artistic advice (Dee) and a welcome distraction (Kasper) xx

**JOIN ONE TINY BIRD ON A HILARIOUS ADVENTURE TO
SAVE HIS SISTER - AND HIS COUNTRY!**

'Full of adventure and heart'
Cressida Cowell, bestselling author of
HOW TO TRAIN YOUR DRAGON

'Magnificent fun'
David Walliams, bestselling author of
CODE NAME BANANAS

DERMOT O'LEARY

WINGS OF GLORY

HE'S FAST!
HE'S BRAVE!
HE'S A SUPER
POOPER!

ILLUSTRATED BY CLAIRE POWELL

**ALSO AVAILABLE AS AN AUDIO BOOK,
READ BY DERMOT HIMSELF.**

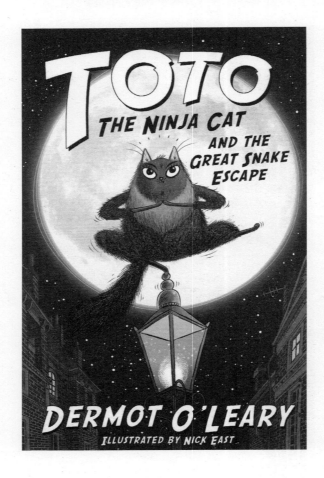

TOTO
THE NINJA CAT
AND THE INCREDIBLE CHEESE HEIST

DERMOT O'LEARY

ILLUSTRATED BY NICK EAST

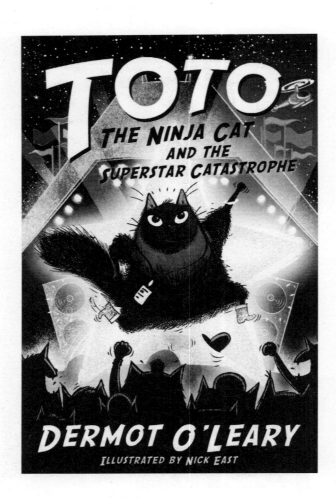

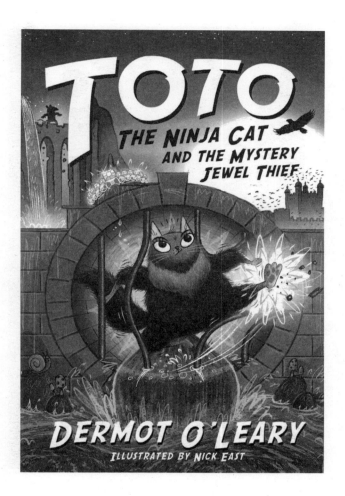

TOTO
THE NINJA CAT
AND THE MYSTERY JEWEL THIEF

DERMOT O'LEARY
ILLUSTRATED BY NICK EAST

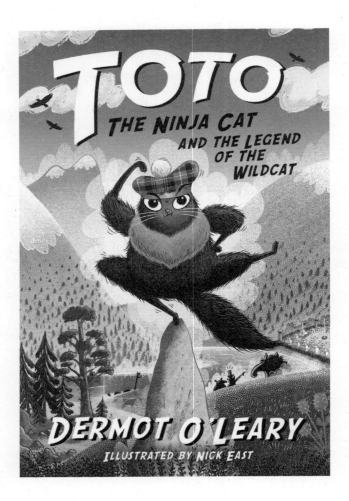

TOTO
THE NINJA CAT
AND THE LEGEND OF THE WILDCAT

DERMOT O'LEARY

ILLUSTRATED BY NICK EAST

THEY'RE ALSO AVAILABLE AS AUDIO BOOKS,
READ BY DERMOT HIMSELF!

TURN THE PAGE TO FIND OUT WHAT HAPPENED
WHEN *TOTO THE NINJA CAT* BEGAN HER FIRST
TOTALLY PAWSOME ADVENTURE . . .

JOIN TOTO THE NINJA CAT AND HER BROTHER, SILVER, AS THEY BEGIN THEIR FIRST ADVENTURE IN LONDON. THEY'VE JUST MOVED TO THE BIG CITY FROM A TINY VILLAGE IN ITALY, AND THEIR NEW FRIEND, CATFACE, HAS BEEN SHOWING THEM AROUND. BUT DANGER IS AFOOT - READ ON TO FIND OUT MORE . . .

As the cats stepped off the Tube at Camden Town, not far from Regent's Park, it was clear that the parakeets had good reason to be hysterical. What had been a sleepy, tranquil night was now pandemonium. There were animals everywhere! The local dogs were barking (which in animal language is just shouting the same thing over and over again) and trying to get out of their gardens; the neighbourhood cats were hanging around the street corners, chatting loudly and looking moody. Birds of all sorts – blackbirds, pigeons, robins, tits – were swooping through the sky, making more noise than the rest of the animals put together. Even a couple of hedgehogs had emerged from a nearby bush, looking a bit sleepy and confused.

CAMDEN WAS IN ANIMAL CHAOS!

'Robert, what on earth is happening?' Catface asked a passing parakeet.

'You sure you want to know?' the bird replied, perching on top of a gate. 'It's the zoo. We flew over there about an hour ago, and the whole place is in uproar ... *BRIAN HAS ESCAPED!*'

CHAPTER 4

'BRIAN? ESCAPED? BRIAN? HOW CAN
THIS BE? IT'S IMPOSSIBLE!' ranted Catface,
his face sheet-white.

Toto and Silver looked at each other
blankly. *Brian?*

'This is a disaster! We'll have to evacuate
the whole of Camden now!' Catface
continued. 'Thank you, Robert. Best of luck,
eh. Are you heading out of town?'

'Don't worry about me,' chirped Robert. 'I've got these bad boys,' he said, flapping his wings. 'I can fly – Brian can't. It's you guys who need to worry – he'll be coming this way for sure. I'm off to squawk at more animals!'

'This is bad, kids, as bad as it gets,' said Catface. 'We are in deep doo-doo.'

Silver fell about laughing. 'Deep doo-doo! Brilliant. Toto, he said *DOO-DOO!*'

'My friends, you don't understand,' said Catface. 'We *have* to get you two safely home. Then I must be on my way, back to my family to warn them, and then I think I might make for the country ... high ground – Scotland, perhaps. I've got more family there. I can get the morning train and be there by lunchtime ...'

'I'm sorry,' said Toto, 'but **WHO IS BRIAN?** And why is everyone so scared of someone called ... *Brian*?'

'Listen very carefully,' said Catface. 'You have no idea what Brian is capable of. He's clever, he's silent, and he is almost impossible for humans to catch. Brian is the stuff of legend, a ghost story that mummy animals tell their kids to make them behave. *"If you don't eat all your dinner, Brian will come and gobble you up."* Only it's not a made-up story, it's true! If he comes this way, which he will, as there are so many of us to ... *gobble* ... we're all doomed. We have to get you inside.'

'But what *is* Brian?' asked Toto.

'Brian,' sighed Catface, 'is a snake. And no ordinary snake ... He is the famous King Cobra of London Zoo, one of the deadliest snakes in the world. Everyone has feared this day from the moment he was given a home there. Now that he has escaped, he will eat whatever he finds: birds, snakes, you, me. He will then try to mate and have babies—'

'UGH, GROSS!' exclaimed Silver.

'Thanks for that,' continued Catface. 'If he finds a lady cobra, and there are many in captivity around London, they will have forty or fifty babies, and do you know who *they* will eat? **ALL OF US**.'

'But ... he's called *Brian*. He doesn't sound *that* scary,' said Silver.

'I know,' replied Catface. 'It's a ridiculous name. I'm sure it was given to him to make him sound a bit cuddly and friendly, two things he absolutely isn't. Now, back to your house, you two, and don't come out again until he is caught.'

'You said he's impossible for humans to catch. Why don't we have a go?' asked Toto.

'Have you taken leave of your senses?' asked Catface. 'He's one of the most dangerous animals on the planet, and you want to go off on some adventure to find him? And just suppose we do track him down, what then? I can't fight him – no one can. We have to get to safety *now*.'

They trudged back to the house where they had started their night-time adventure only a few hours before. Catface was about to help them over the gate, when Toto turned around, a steely look in her eye.

'Listen,' said Toto. 'This is your home, right? If you run now, you'll never come back. We've just got here, and we love it already. Yes, it's a bit cold, and your pasta is nowhere near as good as ours, but look at this street. All the animals live happily alongside each other. This is our home and I for one want to fight for it. So I'm not running away—'

'Sis, you can't run away,' Silver interrupted. 'You can't see where you're going.'

'Not helpful,' replied Toto. 'But yes, I wouldn't actually be able to see exactly where I was going, thank you, Silver.'

'You're welcome,' he said.

'So, what's it to be, Catface? Will you help us, and will you let us help you?'

Catface sighed, and smiled at the two little cats. 'Look, I'm a coward. I don't like fighting, and there is no way – **NO WAY** – we can defeat the awesome power of Brian. But if you insist on trying to capture him, then ... oh, I can't believe I'm saying this ... then I'll help. We'll have to start at the zoo to find out where he's headed. Oh my, we're all going to get eaten!'

'Keep it light, Catface,' said Silver. 'So, you're in?'

'I'm in,' said Catface.

'Good,' said Silver. 'Because we have no idea where the zoo is.'

Catface, of course, knew exactly where to go.

DERMOT O'LEARY is the bestselling author of the
Toto the Ninja Cat series, which has sold hundreds of thousands
of copies and been translated into sixteen languages.
His extensive career across the television, radio and entertainment
industries has established him as a household name. Dermot is
currently seen presenting ITV's *This Morning* alongside Alison
Hammond every Friday. When not entertaining viewers through
the telly, Dermot can be found via the radio waves as he kicks off
the weekend for listeners on *The Dermot O'Leary Show* on BBC
Radio 2. He's fronted shows including *The X Factor*, *The NTAs*
and *The Earthshot Prize Awards*, a BAFTA- and RTS-winning
event that was set up by The Royal Foundation.
He has always been passionate about history and has fronted and
produced documentaries such as *Battle of Britain: The Day the War
Was Won*, *Return of the Spitfires* and *48 Hours to Victory*. When he's
not got his head in a history book, he enjoys time with his son
and an afternoon at the Arsenal, or a nice wild swim.

CLAIRE POWELL is a *New York Times* bestselling children's book illustrator, who has worked on many chart-topping books with authors such as Kes Gray and Simon Farnaby. *The Swifts*, written by Beth Lincoln, was an instant *New York Times* bestseller and *The King's Birthday Suit*, by Peter Bentley, was nominated for the Lollies award in 2023.